Moonlight

(The Moon Trilogy)
Book 1

Tim O'Rourke

Story Editor
Lynda O'Rourke
Book cover designed by:
Suzi Midnight
Copyright: Suzi Midnight 2012
suzimidnightsun@bigpond.com
Edited by:
Carolyn M. Pinard
carolynpinardconsults@gmail.com
www.thesupernaturalbookeditor.com

Dedicated to Michelle Auricht who makes a great BETA reader and an even better flesh eating Vampire!

More books by Tim O'Rourke

Vampire Shift (Kiera Hudson Series 1) Book 1
Vampire Wake (Kiera Hudson Series 1) Book 2
Vampire Hunt (Kiera Hudson Series 1) Book 3
Vampire Breed (Kiera Hudson Series 1) Book 4
Wolf House (Kiera Hudson Series 1) Book 4.5
Vampire Hollows (Kiera Hudson Series 1) Book 5
Dead Flesh (Kiera Hudson Series 2) Book 1
Dead Night (Kiera Hudson Series 2) Book 1.5
Dead Angels (Kiera Hudson Series 2) Book 2
Black Hill Farm (Book 1)
Black Hill Farm: Andy's Diary (Book 2)
Doorways (Doorways Trilogy Book 1)
The League of Doorways (Doorways Trilogy Book 2)

You can contact Tim O'Rourke at
www.Ravenwoodgreys.com
Or by email at Ravenwoodgreys@aol.com

Prologue

"Don't hurt me," the girl sobbed, mascara-stained tears striping her cheeks.

"Shhh," he whispered in her ear, liking the sound of her heart beating against him. It had all been so easy. She had come with him just like that. Girls like her always did. The ones with the low self-esteem, the girls who sat alone in the corner of the nightclub while their friends danced in the centre of the dance floor. Men hovering around them like flies around shit. They were all shit. However, the girls in the corners were different.

They would giggle as he complimented them. They weren't used to that – it embarrassed them – but boy did they enjoy hearing what he had to say. Of course they did – no one paid them compliments – no one noticed them, they were hidden in the corner. He noticed them though, he had noticed her.

She trembled before him, wishing now that she hadn't had so much to drink. Her knees didn't knock together because of the Smirnoff Ice the guy had plied her with. They knocked together out of fear. She had never been naked in front of anyone before – she'd never had reason to. No one had asked her to take off her clothes like he had. His voice had been soft – coaxing – as her dress fell to the floor. At first she had giggled and covered her flesh with her arms, but he had gently pulled them away. That gorgeous smile of his had told her that it was okay - he liked her - he really did.

Oh, yes.

He eyed her. So much flesh, he smiled to himself. Enough to go around.

"Please just let me call my mum," the girl sobbed in his arms.

He held her gently and smelt the fear which leaked from her in waves. His heart quickened just like hers.

"My roommate will be back soon," the girl whispered, squirming against his smooth chest. She secretly knew that her friend wouldn't be home until morning, and by then, she would be dead. She knew that and she wanted her mum. Just to speak to her, to hear her voice one last time. "Please..." she whispered, looking up into his dark eyes.

His eyes hadn't been so dark in the nightclub. Back there, they had twinkled as he had flirted with her as he had whispered all the things that she'd always longed a boy would whisper to her. His mouth had been different, too. In the unlit corner of the nightclub, his lips had felt soft like new-born skin as they had brushed over her cheek, making her skin tingle. Now, in the gloom of her room, his lips seemed to have stretched somehow, as if pulled up behind his ears, and all the girl could think of was Heath Ledger disguised as the Joker.

It wasn't just the guy's lips; it was what lay behind them that told the girl she would never hear her mum's voice again. The two ivory-looking points jutted from his black gums like blades.

There was a noise and the girl glanced up. It was the sound of her bedroom door being pushed open. She was saved; her roommate was back already! She peered over his shoulder and looked towards the open doorway, her eyes brimming with hope.

"Who are you?" she breathed, she was now wanting her heart to stop and put an end to the suffering she knew was going to come.

The figures standing in the open doorway stepped into the room. Both were young, no older than twenty-five. One male, one female. They ignored her question and spoke to the other.

"You have done well," the male said, his lips seeming to spread up and open across his face, revealing a set of razor-sharp teeth.

"I haven't come to talk," the female said. "I'm ravenous."

With his arms still wrapped around the trembling girl, the man looked back at the others, and with a smile, he said, "Let's eat then."

The girl closed her eyes at the sight of the freaky-looking mouths which lunged at her. A warm sensation raced through her body, and with it came a numbness and total darkness.

The three of them fed. They gorged themselves until they could eat no more.

Chapter One

Thaddeus Blake sat with his back to the river and spied through the heavy traffic. He watched the young girl, who sat hunched on the steps of the Embankment Tube Station. The February evening was bitter, and Thaddeus Blake watched as she tucked her dirty hands into the sleeves of her worn sweater. This was the seventh night he had spent sitting across the road from her, looking on as she implored the passing commuters to part with some spare change. Most ignored her whilst looking straight through her skeletal frame. The odd few did toss her coins, but others, usually older men, would pause beside her as they shared a few discreet words. The girl would become angry and start to shout at them. Her words were drowned out by the sound of passing night buses and taxis.

Sometimes, when she collected enough for food or a drink, she would disappear. Thaddeus would continue to wait in the dark, neatly dressed in a near black suit, crisp white shirt, with a blood-red silk tie. Hands laced in lap, legs crossed at the ankles, he would wait for her to return. She always did, sometimes after only a few minutes where she would resume her position on the steps. On two occasions she had been accompanied by a younger girl - fourteen-years-old, perhaps? He couldn't be sure. She was scruffy-looking too - but unlike the other, the younger girl would sometimes sway on her feet, toppling over and collapsing onto the ground, consumed by drugs or alcohol - probably both.

But tonight, the older girl who had fascinated him so much was alone and having a rougher time than usual as she sat curled up, rocking back and forth in the cold. The commuters passed her by in busy streams, seeking the warmth of pubs, clubs, or the warmth of their lover's bed. Thaddeus pulled up the sleeve of his suit and read the time. It was just past eight. He would give it another two hours or so, and then he would approach the girl.

Thaddeus spent the next two hours dining at a restaurant just off Trafalgar Square. For a man of medium build, he could be known to eat a hearty meal, and tonight he had put away two very rare sirloin steaks with a side order of ham, a large plate of fried potatoes and sweet peas, finished off with a giant serving of blueberry pie. As a rule, he drank very little, wanting - always needing - to keep his wits about him. But tonight he had consumed three glasses of red wine. After his meal, he sat for a short time, smoking a cigarette in the dimly-lit restaurant with the smell and taste of fresh tobacco curling up from his full lips and lingering around his slender fingers.

He arrived back on the opposite side of the road from the Embankment Tube Station at just past ten. A chill wind had picked up and it ran its icy fingers through his messy-looking hair. He spied the young girl, who was still there, now standing faint and tired-looking against the white stone of the building. Thaddeus lingered for several minutes more, then gracefully crossed the road at the traffic lights and approached the girl.

She stood facing away from him, her long, matted hair whispering about her shoulders and hiding most of her face. Thaddeus came alongside her and stopped. Feeling his presence, she turned, and through her long fringe, looked up into his face. She figured on first sight that he couldn't be more than twenty-five years in age, but he could have been older. It was his eyes, she thought. They were two dark brown spheres, set deeply into his face. They were alive and sparkling in the light from passing traffic. They generated such life, they made the rest of his face look worn and tired somehow. The pallor of his skin was so very pale, she wondered if he were not ill. His lips were full in colour though, so very dark. A wave of untidy hair framed his face. It didn't look a mess by accident; he had styled it that way. The lower half of his face was covered in a few days' stubble, which had been neatly trimmed.

After what seemed like time unknown, she broke her study of the stranger's face and moved slightly away from him. She wasn't scared, but she knew these city types would rather not be seen with a tart, even if they did try and buy sex from her. That was a secret they kept hidden away in the backs of cabs, cheap hotel rooms, down infested alleyways, where if they could, they would leave her with their dirty secrets and return home to clean sheets and their even cleaner wives. She knew a lot of girls - and some boys - who did such things. Not her though - not ever. She would rather have starved.

Looking away from him, she said, "What do you want, mister?"

Still looking at her, Thaddeus replied, "Just a few hours of your time."

No one had ever asked her for a few hours before, and she became a little nervous. She hid it well and said, "Get lost, mister. I'm not for sale."

"Money isn't a problem, whatever you ask," he said back, his eyes still fixed on her, and even in the bitterly cold wind he could smell her. It was a musty, sweaty, unclean smell, and he wanted to cover his nose with his hand.

She felt nervous; something wasn't right. The girl couldn't help but wonder why this well-to-do type was offering her money like this, when all he had to do was call up an agency and get himself a proper tart.

"No, sorry, mister, that sorta thing isn't my bag."

Thaddeus smiled and said, "Why? Have you got yourself a better offer?" He laughed softly into the evening but not mockingly.

"Look, why don't you fuck-off? I said I ain't interested, didn't I?" she snapped at him.

She had her back to him, but he could sense the fear in her voice. Thaddeus felt ashamed; he hadn't meant to scare her. So he spoke to her again, but this time soothingly, his voice like a song against the steady hiss of traffic. "Look, I'm sorry if I have upset you, no harm was meant. I would just like to pay you for the privilege of your company for the next few hours."

The young girl listened to the sound of his voice, rather than what he was saying. She was caught by it. For a moment she was entranced by the sound of it. After mere seconds, she pulled herself together and wheeled around to face him. "How many ways have I got to tell you? I ain't gonna screw you, however posh you talk with all your fancy words!"

Thaddeus never broke his gaze, eyes locked onto hers as if they couldn't, or wouldn't let go. He spoke softly to her again.

"I never said I wanted to bed you. Quite the opposite, in fact. All I want to do is buy you dinner and talk." Then showing her the palms of his hands, as if to prove she had no reason to fear him, he smiled again and said, "Just talk."

She broke his stare for the second time that evening and rocked her head back, spilling laughter into the night. "Yeah, right! You want to buy me dinner. Now I really have heard it all. I've been given some bullshit in my time, but that...."

"Look, I am being straight with you," Thaddeus cut in, his voice was sincere as he held her gaze again. "I have no interest in having sex with you of any kind. I have no intention of harming you in any way. We can eat wherever you wish. I just want to talk to you."

The young girl felt the sincerity in his voice, and believed she saw it
in those eyes of his . She felt drawn by them, could feel herself soften and weaken. The thought of a good meal sent her stomach into hungry convulsions. She spoke to him, this time calmer.

"What do you want to talk about?"

Knowing he had her, he took her gently by the arm and led her up to the Strand. "You eat first," he said, "then I talk."

As they moved off, a very odd-looking couple but completely unnoticed in London, she thought whatever it was he wanted to talk about, she could listen to his voice all night long.

Chapter Two

Fifteen minutes later, Thaddeus Blake was sitting opposite the young girl in a pizza parlour. He watched with some amusement as she forked large helpings of pasta into her hungry mouth. She washed every forkful down with a gulp of milk, leaving a white fringe across her upper lip. Thaddeus looked on with fascination as he smoked and drank a large mugful of sweet black coffee. Both the bitter scent of the coffee beans and the tobacco smoke, which lingered around his fingers, masked the stench that wafted across the table from the girl. As he pitched his cigarette out into the ashtray, she spoke to him through a mouthful of food.

"You said you wanted to talk. Go on then." She knocked her fringe from her eyes, and Thaddeus noticed two things that pleased him. Although her hair was matted with dirt and grime, he could see that if it was washed, it would blaze a bright copper. What pleased him more than anything, were her eyes. Thaddeus knew that with some rest and healthy living, they would shine a beautiful green. Her lips were pale, seemingly bloodless, but with a strong cupid's bow.

"How old are you?" he questioned her.

She replied quickly without looking up from the plate of food. "Twenty-one."

"Truthfully, please," he asked again.

This time she did look up at him and met his gaze. "Eighteen."

Thaddeus nodded and spoke again, "Friends or family?"

She took another swig of the milk, swallowed hard, and then said, "Are you taking the piss?"

"Sorry," Thaddeus said, regretting his naive line of questioning.

"I've been in care for as long as I can remember," she said. "It wasn't so great. So I did a bunk when I was fourteen and came to London. Been here pretty much ever since."

"Drugs?" Thaddeus asked.

"No thanks," she said, forking more of the pasta into her mouth.

"I wasn't offering them to you," he shot back. "Do you take them?"

"I've done a lot of stuff I'm not necessarily proud of," she said, staring at him across the table, "but I've never done no drugs."

Then leaning across the table, Thaddeus gripped hold of her left wrist and forced back the sleeve of her shabby sweater to the crook of her elbow.

"Hey!" she barked, "What the fuck are you doing?"

Thaddeus looked at her pale arm. The skin was milky-white and unblemished. "I'm sorry," he said, and released her arm.

"No drugs, and no sex," she whispered, and pulled down her sleeve. Then fixing him with an angry stare, she added, "I know your type. You think that everyone who is homeless is a drug-taking whore."

"I'm sorry," Thaddeus said, and an uncomfortable silence fell over the table. Thaddeus lit another cigarette as he watched the girl. When he had smoked it down almost to his knuckle, he said, "What's your name?"

"Winter McCall," she said, forking the last of the pasta into her mouth.

"Winter? Is that some kind of street name?" he asked her, feeling slightly amused.

She saw the smile tugging at the corner of his lips, and said, "No, it's my real name. Apparently I was born during the middle of the worst snowstorm in years. The snow was so deep that the ambulance got stuck before reaching the hospital. I was born in the back of the ambulance, so my mum called me Winter. Most people just call me Winnie."

"What do you prefer?" Thaddeus asked her.

"I don't care much," she shrugged, staring out of the window, wondering how long it would be before she was forced out into the cold again. Then, looking back at the stranger who had bought her dinner, Winnie said, "So what's your story? What's your name?"

"My name is Thaddeus Blake, and I'd like you to work for me," he said, then swilled down the rest of his coffee.

"Sorry, mister," Winnie said, standing to leave. "I don't need no pimp."

Thaddeus moved with lightning grace and took hold of her hand before she could leave. "I didn't mean that. I wouldn't be so vulgar to offer you such a proposition. The work isn't of that nature."

Winnie looked down into his eyes and saw the openness, that honesty she had seen before on the steps of the Embankment. He spoke again, his voice gentle as always, "Please stay a while and listen to what I have to say, and if when I am finished you still want to leave, then you won't get any more harassments from me."

He let go of her hand. Winnie stood between the chair and the table. She looked down at the stranger before her and felt confused. On one hand he seemed strong and slightly arrogant, but on the other hand, he seemed gentle and a little naive. He implored her once more, his voice barely a whisper.

"Please trust me. Stay a little longer. You can go at any time. I am true to my word."

Those last two words Winnie had heard so many times before in her life, and too often they had meant very little. For reasons she couldn't quite explain, Winnie found herself taking her seat once more on the opposite side of the table. Somehow, she felt strangely in control of the situation. She sensed a certain desperateness about Thaddeus Blake which he fought to keep hidden beneath his cool exterior.

"Okay, I'm listening," she said, "but any funny stuff, and I'm gone, mister."

"Please, call me Thaddeus," he smiled warmly.

Winnie eyed him cautiously and said, "So what kind of job are you offering?"

Thaddeus drew a silver flip case from his breast pocket, opened it, and offered a cigarette to Winnie.

"It's not a habit I can afford," she said, waving the case away with her grubby hand.

Thaddeus put the case away after taking one for himself and lit it. Once settled, he spoke.

"I'd like you to come and work for me at my home in Cornwall. In the last year, I have purchased a big home there, which takes a great deal of looking after and care. All I'd ask of you is to keep it clean. Your other duties would be to prepare my meals and do my laundry."

Winnie watched him blow smoke out of his nostrils as she said, "Ever thought about getting yourself a wife, mister. Or a maid?"

"I've had both. My wife died almost a year ago of cancer, and the maid just didn't work out."

"A wife?" Winnie asked, unable to mask her surprise. "You must have married young. You can't be any older than twenty-five."

"We met as teenagers," he said, turning as if to watch the people pass in the street outside. "From the very first time I saw her, I loved her."

Winnie watched his pale reflection in the window and said, "I'm sorry that you weren't together longer. She must have died very young."

"The time we spent together was very special - it felt like an eternity," he whispered, looking back at Winnie.

Not knowing what to say next, and embarrassed by Thaddeus's obvious sadness, Winnie said, "So why didn't the whole maid thing work out?"

Thaddeus stubbed out his cigarette, which was only half-smoked, and laced his hands over each other on the table. "I have become somewhat of a recluse. I keep myself to myself. I tend to keep strange hours, mostly sleeping during the day and working through the night. It just got too much for my maid. She was old, and fetching my meals during the night and changing my linen became too much, and we parted company."

"Ever thought about changing your sleeping pattern?" Winnie asked dryly, eyeing him from beneath her matted fringe. "It might work wonders for your social life."

"Let's just say I prefer the moonlight," he smiled wistfully. "Besides, after my wife's death, I had what you might call a breakdown. It wasn't my mind which was broken - it was my heart. I shied away from people and the daylight, and all that it offered in its bright and harsh clarity. I prefer the nights. They are quieter and full of peace, with everybody away in bed. I can come and go as I please without being disturbed. The world seems mine then, and mine alone. As I have said, I work at night and I find the peace it gives me refreshing."

"What's your work?"

"I'm a writer; a poet in fact," Thaddeus explained. "So as I'm sure you'll understand, I enjoy the solitude of the night. It sounds a little pretentious, I know, but I prefer to work that way."

"Okay, mister, but..." Winnie started.

"Please, call me Thaddeus," he reminded her with a smile.

"Okay, Thaddeus," she said, "but what you've said doesn't explain a great deal. Why choose me? I'm a beggar, living on the streets of London, without anything to offer. To be honest, I can barely read and write..."

Before she'd had a chance to finish talking herself out of the job offer, Thaddeus cut over her and said, "I've been in London over this last week visiting with my publishers, and each evening it has been my wish to walk along the river. Each night when I've reached the Embankment, there you have been, begging and being sneered at by strangers. Don't get me wrong; I'm not offering you pity or charity. If you do decide to come back to Cornwall with me, you'll be working hard for your keep. As I have already pointed out, I do have some strange habits, and perhaps a few requests from time to time that you might think a little odd, but let me assure you once again, I don't want you for sex of any sort."

Winnie looked across the table at him and asked bluntly, "Are you gay?"

"No, I'm not gay," Thaddeus said, with a smile. "As I have already explained, I've been married. I loved my wife very dearly and she will never be replaced."

Winnie watched him. She had become good at people watching during the many hours she had spent begging outside railway stations, and she couldn't help but notice how his eyes grew almost black as he spoke of his wife. It was more than just sadness she could see in them; it was despair.

"How much will you be paying me?" she asked, changing the subject.

"You'll have your own private room. All food and any other extras will be paid for," Thaddeus explained. "You won't have to pay any bills. I'll give you two hundred pounds per week, to spend in whatever way you see fit, as long as you are there when I need you, and are willing to succumb to any other little request I might make of you."

Winnie swallowed hard. Two hundred a week. Lately, she'd been lucky if she'd scrounged two pounds a week from begging. Money aside, she was still wary of Thaddeus Blake. She only knew what he had chosen to tell her about himself.

"Two hundred a week, huh?" she said, pulling the ends of her sleeves down over her dirty hands. "A big house in the country... I didn't know anyone could make so much money from writing down a few fancy words that rhyme."

Thaddeus laughed and said, "I wish my poems made me money, they only make a fraction of my income - just pocket money, really. No, my wealth has been inherited. Like I have explained, I am the last and have no one to share it with – unless, that is, if you take me up on my offer."

Winnie looked back at him across the table and said nothing.

"What have you got to lose, Winnie?" he asked.

Again, she said nothing and just stared into his brown eyes.

"I have been honest with you," he shrugged, as if now the whole thing was not so important after all. "It's up to you. No pressure. I have kept to my side of the bargain. I bought you dinner and we talked."

Sensing that her opportunity of escaping London and the evils she had discovered there was may be slipping away, she whispered, "How can I be sure that I can trust you?"

Thaddeus looked Winnie squarely in the face and said, "You won't know unless you come back to Cornwall with me."

Then pushing his chair back from the table, he added, "The hour is getting late. I'll be leaving tomorrow evening at seven from Paddington Railway Station. If you wish to take up my offer, meet me on the concourse and we shall leave together. If you chose not to meet me, I shall go back to my home and forget this meeting, and you."

They parted company outside the pizza parlour, Winnie making her way back to the Embankment. After she was out of sight, Thaddeus hailed a taxi and disappeared off into the night. To him, the night was still very young, and he had a lot to do before dawn.

Chapter Three

Winnie made her way back to the Embankment. It was close to midnight now, not that time meant much to her. The days, nights, and hours all just rolled into one. Normally there was no break from the constant feel of hunger that gnawed away at her insides. Tonight she didn't feel hungry; her shrunken stomach felt bloated, and it was a feeling that she had forgotten even existed. People poured out of the clubs and pubs, but they were nothing but ghosts to her. Or was it the other way around? She wondered. Was she the ghost? No one ever seemed to notice her, unless she made a complete nuisance of herself by thrusting her filthy hands under their noses, and asking for any spare change that they might have. Some gave her the loose coins they had jingling in their pockets, but others just looked away, their noses turned up. She didn't really blame them. Winnie knew she looked more like an animal than a human. Her hair was plastered with dirt, and her clothes were threadbare and just as dirty as her skin. Thanks to the city worker who thought it would be amusing to take a piss over her as she lay huddled in a shop doorway three nights ago, she now stank of urine, too.

Winnie reached the Embankment, and she could hear the sound of the water slosh against the shore. Party boats cruised over the black water of the Thames, the sound of muffled laughter and music being carried on the wind. Late night trains rattled over Blackfriars Bridge, taking the last of the commuters home for the night, just to turn around and come back again in a few hours' time and start all over. Drawing her hands up into the sleeves of her sweater, she felt the two bread rolls she had sneaked from the pizza bar. They weren't for her - they were for her friend, Ruby Little. Winnie didn't know her real name and she wondered if Ruby could still remember it herself. She was named Ruby because of the dirty red coat she always wore. Little, because she was *little*. It wasn't any more complex than that. However, Ruby was more than just *little*. She was fragile - like one of those china statues Winnie had often seen in the posh shops in Knightsbridge.

But what Winnie couldn't figure out was if Ruby was indeed a friend. She wasn't sure. Winnie cared for her - perhaps like a younger sister. Ruby could be trouble, though. Winnie knew that Ruby had stolen from her before - the little money she had managed to scrounge that day - Ruby had sometimes sneaked from her pocket while she had been sleeping. Ruby was just as hungry as her, but what pissed Winnie off, was that she spent the money on blow, or worse. Ruby was cracked out of her skull most of the time, and would need looking after. Winnie didn't always have time for that. Begging was a fulltime occupation. Hours spent watching over Ruby while she lay choking on her own vomit was time Winnie could spend hustling for money - money that would buy her more survival time. Even though Ruby would sometimes steal from her, she was company - someone to talk to when the nights were just too cold to sleep. Winnie had forgotten how many freezing cold nights they spent cuddled together for warmth over the last few years.

But Winnie knew that stealing from her wasn't the only way that Ruby made money. She turned tricks for the men who approached her. Winnie knew why - she knew why most of the girls and boys went with those men - they were feeding a hunger far worse than starvation - they were feeding their drug habit. Winnie had smoked some weed from time to time, but nothing more. There was no coming back when you had taken a step down that darker road. It wasn't food you were begging and stealing for anymore. You needed lots of money to satisfy that particular hunger - the kind of money you only made by selling yourself.

Winnie didn't want to go there - not ever. She would rather die. She had been used before by someone who claimed to have loved her.

In the glare of the night buses, Winnie darted across the busy road and cut across the small concourse of the Embankment Tube Station. The flush of warm air inside momentarily coloured her cheeks. Then she was back in the cold again, and heading left into the archways which ran under the bridge. During the day it was a busy thoroughfare, but as the moon rose and the city went to bed, the archways became a makeshift town of cardboard boxes, soiled blankets, and huddled bodies. Winnie stepped over the seemingly lifeless bodies in search of Ruby. There was a small alcove where Ruby usually slept, but peering into the darkness, Winnie could see that it was empty. She moved forward, one of the others curled beneath the arches had a dog, and it licked dirty drain water from the gutter. It made a yelping noise as Winnie passed by in the dark.

Then, Winnie saw what looked like a heap of red blankets lying in the gutter just ahead. She approached them, and realised that it wasn't a pile of blankets that she could see, but Ruby's red coat. With the sound of her scuffed-out trainers snapping against the cobbled road beneath the arches, Winnie ran towards her friend. Ruby lay on her side, one arm jutting out from beneath her. Her small head was tilted forward, her chin resting against her chest.

"Hey, Ruby," Winnie said. "I've got you something."

Ruby didn't move, even though she had her eyes wide open.

"Look what I've got you," Winnie said, taking the rolls from her threadbare sleeves.

Ruby stayed still, not even her eyelids flickered.

Winnie crouched beside the girl, and it was then that she saw the thick stream of vomit trailing from the corner of her mouth. It was crusty-looking, and bubbles of dried snot blocked Ruby's nostrils.

"Hey, Ruby," Winnie said, shaking her friend gently by the shoulder.

Ruby's head flopped to one side and Winnie stared into her blank eyes. Her lips were mauve, the skin around them blue. Winnie knew that it wasn't just the freezing cold which had turned them that colour.

"Ruby?" Winnie whispered, shaking her friend again.

Ruby just stared back at her, her eyes blank - dead.

With tears standing in her eyes, the two bread rolls fell from Winnie's hands and into the gutter. There was a woofing noise as the dog leapt forward and snatched them away in its jaws.

Then gently, as if handling one of those china statues, Winnie lifted Ruby into her arms and cradled her dead body.

"Somebody help me!" Winnie cried out loud, but the only response she got was the dog barking back at her from somewhere in the darkness. Winnie knew she had lost her only companion, however difficult she could be at times.

"Please somebody help me," she sobbed, but she knew nobody would.

Winnie looked into Ruby's upturned face, and the line of ropey vomit made her look as if she was smiling somehow. "I'm scared," Winnie whispered. "I'm so scared."

But not because of the hideous grin spread across the dead girl's face, but because she knew that one day, however hard she tried not to succumb to the same nightmares that Ruby had lived, she, too, would end up dead. Winnie wasn't scared of dying - it was how she died that she feared. She didn't want to die like Ruby had; choking on the drugs which had been bought with the money she had got for selling her body. That was no way to live and no way to die.

But what choice did she have? And then she thought of the offer Thaddeus Blake had made her.

Chapter Four

Thaddeus Blake had arisen from his hotel bed at five, just before dusk. He showered and dressed himself in a black turtleneck sweater, dark denims, and a deep blue jacket. On leaving the hotel, he had made his way to Oxford Street and purchased some clothes for his new traveling companion. He had no doubt in his mind that Winnie would be at Paddington Railway Station. Thaddeus had chosen a violet top, jeans and boots. As he lingered over the garments, he pictured Winnie in the clothes he had selected for her. He pictured her seething locks of copper hair bouncing delicately off the violet top. Thaddeus could also see her enchanting emerald eyes, enhanced by the colour of her hair. She was going to look perfect for what he had in mind for her. Underwear came next, selecting a pair of panties and bra. Then there was the smell - Winnie's smell. It wasn't her fault, he knew, but it was pungent and turned his stomach. So he chose some shampoo, soap, and perfume. Thaddeus paid for all the items in cash and left the store.

He now stood on the concourse at Paddington Station, a little before seven o'clock. The carrier bag with the clothes and his own leather suitcase sat neatly by his feet as he waited for Winnie to arrive. He watched the throng of commuters who waited restlessly, looking up at the luminous displays, checking to see what platform their train home that night would depart from.

Others seemed more relaxed and sat on heaped mounds of luggage, drinking from soda cans and chewing on cheaply-made sandwiches. The homeless continued to beg, and pigeons circled above in the diesel fumes which belched from the engines of departing trains. Thaddeus had no love for the city, and he longed to be back at home in the clean air and the safety of his sanctuary.

Without even noticing her arrive, Winnie had crept up beside him.

"What time does our train leave?" she asked him.

He smiled with his eyes and replied, "Seven-thirty."

Winnie stood, arms wrapped about her fragile frame which she hid beneath the same dirty sweater. She also wore the same faded denims as the previous night, which were covered from thigh to calf in grime and dirt. Her feet were clad in worn trainers, which flopped loosely about her feet, due to oversize and lack of laces.

Thaddeus could see at once that Winnie appeared disturbed in some way, and he wondered if she was going to turn and run at any minute. "Are you okay?" he asked her.

Winnie thought of Ruby, the last she had seen of her was being slid into the back of the hearse, zipped tight in a black plastic body bag. The police officers had asked her questions, but not many. It was obvious what had happened. Winnie didn't want to think about that - that was in the past now and she didn't want to go back there. So brushing aside her long, unruly fringe, she looked at Thaddeus and said, "I'm just a bit nervous, that's all."

"You have nothing to be nervous about," he smiled. "I promise." Then, picking up the carrier bag in a quick movement, he handed it to her.

Winnie looked confused.

"It's okay, I bought you some new clothes to travel in," he explained.

"Look, I ain't no charity case. I got my..." she started.

Thaddeus cut across her with a gentle smile dancing over his lips and in his eyes, and said, "Call it an advance on your wages."

Winnie looked down, and pulling open the bag, she peered inside. She raised her eyebrows, and closing it she looked up at him.

"You were that sure that I'd come, you went and bought these clothes?"

Without taking his eyes from her, he said, "I wasn't sure you would come, but I kind of hoped you would." He then took a metal comb from his back trouser pocket and handed it to her. "Go freshen up."

Without looking back, she headed across the concourse in the direction of the female bathrooms where she could have a wash and put on the clean clothes. She had become used to washing in public bathrooms, but at least now she had some decent soap and shampoo to do the job properly. Winnie had also become accustomed to the stares that you got, but today she didn't care. Today she would leave the bathrooms looking as good as any of the other women who stood and preened themselves in the long mirrors above the sinks.

Winnie found the cubicle for disabled people and slipped inside, closing the door behind her. She chose that particular cubicle as they were bigger than the others, and they had their own sink and hand dryer. She could wash and change without others looking at her. Filling a basin with warm water, she leant forward at the waist and wetted her hair the best she could. Winnie squirted some of the shampoo into the palms of her hands and then massaged it into her hair. Leaning forward again, she washed the white foamy suds away. The smell of the shampoo was sweet and almost intoxicating and at once she started to feel better about herself. Then stripping down to her grey underwear, she refilled the sink with clean water.

She washed as best as she could, splashing her arms, legs, and face with water and soap. It felt as if she was washing away the last few years from the pores of her skin. Turning on the automatic dryer, Winnie angled the nozzle so as to dry her hair, face, arms, and legs. Then snatching up the bag of clothes Thaddeus had given her, she pulled them out and dressed.

Alone again, Thaddeus purchased Winnie a ticket from the automated machine. He knew the bag he had given to her contained one of the violet tops, with the black jeans and boots. A fire burnt in his stomach with anticipation as he waited for her to return. He wanted to see if she would look as good as he hoped. After waiting patiently for some time, Thaddeus looked up to see Winnie appear from the ladies bathroom. She came towards him, and his heart beat loud and fast in his chest as he looked on in wonder at the transformation. She was going to be perfect, he thought secretly to himself. The top hung loosely about her frame, shifting and whispering like a violet haze as she moved towards him. He figured her height to be about five-two without the boots, but now she appeared to be much taller. That was good, he thought - it was perfect. He noted that she had put his comb and the shampoo to good use, for her hair now hung in thick, fiery locks about her face and shoulders.

Winnie reached him, feeling fresh and excited in her new clothes. She couldn't remember feeling so good about herself. It was as if she was a person again.

"How do I look, Thaddeus?" she asked.

He knew exactly how she looked, and it was better than he could've ever imagined when he first caught sight of her a week ago, begging outside the Embankment Tube Station. Then as coolly as he could, and wanting to hide his own excitement, he looked at Winnie and simply said, "You look okay." He then turned, snatched up his case and made his way across the concourse towards the platform where their train waited.

They boarded a first-class carriage and took their seats. Winnie excitedly sat in the window seat, as Thaddeus took the seat beside her. The train pulled effortlessly out of the station at dead-on seven-thirty in a cloud of oily blue diesel smoke. Winnie reclined her chair and relaxed, letting her heavy eyelids slide shut. Thaddeus turned slightly in his seat and studied her profile for the briefest of moments, then turned away, and as he did, his eyes turned black with horror. Across the gangway sat a man, the Evening Standard newspaper held up before him. Thaddeus read the bold black headline splashed across the front: *"Female student found savaged in bedsit."*

Chapter Five

Their journey to the south west of England passed with little conversation. Winnie had slept most of the five hours away. She found the soft reclining chair just too comfortable. It was the nearest thing to a bed she had slept on for a very long time. She awoke occasionally as the train drew into stations along the route, and she would throw sidelong glances at Thaddeus. He seemed to be restless, strumming his long, slender fingers on the table before them. He stared deeply through the window and out into the night. The window threw back his own reflection, and he seemed to be staring back into his own dark eyes.

At Exeter, Winnie woke with her bladder pleading to be emptied. She pressed the flat of her hand against her tummy in fear of peeing herself. Thaddeus had gone from beside her, and she peered along the gangway in search of him. The aisle disappeared narrowly away in both directions, but she couldn't see Thaddeus. She spied his suitcase above her on the rack, and guessed he couldn't be far. Air whistled through her teeth, as she sighed and got up from her seat in search of the bathroom. The train seesawed back and forth as she passed amongst the rows of seats. There were only several passengers remaining in the carriage. Most were asleep, one or two were reading, and another sipped from a steaming cup of coffee.

The door which separated the carriages slid effortlessly open for her as she passed through. The bathroom door was showing the *engaged* sign and she waited patiently outside, her hand pressed flat against her stomach. Her need to go was desperate now, as she squeezed her muscles tight and pressed her legs together. She bit into her lower lip, draining the blood there. Not knowing for how much longer she could hold on, Winnie inched forward and rapped on the door with her fist, then tugged at the handle. As she pulled, the train lurched, throwing her forward as the toilet door was opened from the inside. Winnie tumbled into the waiting arms of Thaddeus.

"Steady," he whispered, holding her tightly by both shoulders with his hands.

"Sorry, I thought the door was jammed and I'm bursting...." she groaned, her pale cheeks flushing scarlet.

"Well I won't hold you up any longer," he smiled, releasing his grip on her. He slid past, then turning, he smiled back at her and said,

"Would you like a coffee, Winnie?"

Returning his smile, she nodded. "That would be great, thank you."

He turned away from her and she closed the door. Winnie yanked down her jeans and panties, and hitching her top up about her waist, she sighed. Once finished, she pulled up her jeans and rearranged her top. She squeezed some soap from the container on the wall, and washed her hands in the warm water which tossed and tumbled from the tap. Winnie towelled her hands dry and turned to the mirror to straighten her hair, and paused. Several small drops of what looked like blood stained her top across her right shoulder, where Thaddeus had gripped her only moments ago. She dabbed at it with a wet towel, but the blood was sticky, and it just looked worse where she had tried to wipe it away.

Raking her fingers through her hair, she tried to hide the spots of blood which covered her shoulder. Satisfied that they were hidden, she left the bathroom. Returning to her seat, she found Thaddeus with two small cups of black coffee. Once she had sat down again, Winnie glanced down at Thaddeus's hands. He had tied a white-coloured piece of tissue around his right thumb.

"Have you hurt yourself?" she asked, taking a sip of the hot, sweet coffee.

"My cigarette case," he said, placing his hand beneath the table and out of sight. "One of the edges is slightly serrated. I've been meaning to replace it for a while now, so it is my own stupid fault."

"Does it need stitches?" Winnie asked, thinking of the blood that was now on her top.

"It's just fine. I've covered it for the time being. I shall patch it up when I get home." Then, noticing the blotches of blood, he added, "I'm sorry for ruining your top. You look really pretty."

The sudden compliment surprised Winnie, and although it was nice to hear - after all, who didn't like to hear compliments - she felt awkward and didn't know how to respond.

Watching her, Thaddeus said, "Don't worry about the top, I shall replace it."

Then breaking his stare, and feeling her cheeks flush red again, she turned to look out of the window and said, "You don't have to replace it, you've been too kind already."

They arrived at St. Erth Railway Station just after midnight. The bitter night air engulfed them like an icy blanket as they climbed from the train.

They found a taxi easily enough, and it whisked them through the night to their final destination of St. Ives. The taxi driver pulled up short, just before the turnoff where the main road ended and petered out into a narrow, unruly lane. Thaddeus paid the fare as they clambered from the car with their luggage. They stood before the lane as the taxi's taillights disappeared into the distance.

"The cab driver won't take us any further. The lane is too narrow and the wild bracken scratches the car. I can't blame him, the uneven road doesn't help the suspension either," he remarked as he picked up his case and guided her up the lane, leaving the main road and the warm, orange glow of the street lights behind them. Winnie stayed close behind him, then pausing; she looked back at the road. If she was going to back out now, this was her last chance. Where was she to go? She didn't know this part of England. She had never been to Cornwall before. What did she have to go back to? Winnie had come this far. Turning away from the road, Winnie was faced with the total darkness and silence that lay before her. It was in complete contrast to London at night, which had been bright and full of noise, people, and traffic. She had never known such silence and her new surroundings unnerved her. Thaddeus continued to move briskly ahead. Winnie could barely make out his form before her. Guided by the sound of his footfalls on the stony ground beneath them, she stepped forward into the dark and followed him.

Winnie tripped and stumbled in the dark, and she winced out loud as thorns and wild ivy clawed at her like greedy hands. Not once did Thaddeus trip himself up or snag his clothes on the undergrowth, which grew in a frenzy on either side of them. Winnie guessed that they must be climbing up, because her legs began to tire and her calf muscles ached. They must have been walking for twenty minutes or more, her labouring behind, as Thaddeus strode out ahead. She was just about to cry out and plead for a rest, when Thaddeus came to an abrupt halt. There was a sound in the darkness as she heard him loosen a bolt and swing open a gate. Winnie passed through behind him. Thaddeus closed it, and then strode out in front again.

After only a minute or so of walking, Thaddeus stopped again.

Winnie heard him slip a key into a lock, then another, and then the sound of him pushing a door wide open. He disappeared for a moment, and then there was light. Winnie found herself standing before a large house. She guessed the building had to be very old from the little she could see by the light which spilled from within. She passed through the open doorway, leaving the cold and the night behind her. Thaddeus had disappeared. Winnie looked about the vast hallway she now found herself in. The walls were panelled in a rich, deep oak. Doors to rooms led off the hallway. A wide double staircase grew from the centre of the hall and spiralled upwards into the dark like an ancient spine. Thick patterned rugs covered the polished wooden floor. Portraits adorned the walls. She was no artist, and knew very little of history, but she could tell that the pictures had been beautifully painted, and were very old. She looked about for Thaddeus as she clutched the carrier bag to her chest.

"Thaddeus, are you there?" she called out. As the last of her words trailed off into the depths of the enormous house, lights flickered on from the landing above her. Looking up, Winnie saw Thaddeus standing at the top of the stairs.

"Welcome to my home, Winnie. Come up and I shall show you to your room."

She moved across the hallway and climbed the stairs. At the top, Thaddeus led her down a long narrow corridor, stopping outside a door at the far end. Winnie stepped into the room and looked about in wonder. The room was finely furnished with a four-poster bed at its centre. White drawers and cabinets trailed away in either direction from the bed. A beautifully ornate dressing table stood in the far corner with a small, plush velvet-seated stool before it. A bay window, fringed with lace curtains and silk drapes, faced the bed on the opposite side of the room and added to its size. Walk-in wardrobes, carved in the same fashion as the other furniture, followed the line of the wall to the door where Winnie and Thaddeus now stood. Thaddeus stepped into the room and gazed about.

"This is your room, Winnie." He crossed to the far side and swung open an adjoining door. Gesturing into the room, he said, "This is your bathroom."

My own bathroom? Winnie wondered in awe, as she joined Thaddeus. A thick blue carpet covered the floor, and she could tell it was deep and soft as her boots sank into it. A round-shaped bath lay to one side, slightly sunk into the floor. There was also a shower and toilet. More white cabinets and drawers lined the walls. Crisp white towels hung from a rail fixed to the wall.

"Oh, my god, I can't believe this is going to be my room, it beats the Embankment any day."

Thaddeus caught her gaze and grinned, "Well don't say anything, just enjoy."

Winnie went back into the bedroom and Thaddeus followed.

"It's just that I get the feeling..." Winnie started.

"That it's all too good to be true," he cut in. "That I must have an ulterior motive for having you here?" He looked straight at her, his face blank, not giving anything away. Then, turning, Thaddeus went to the bedroom door. He stopped and faced her again. "I've given you my reasons and you decided to come. If you want to stay, do so, but if you feel you must leave, then go. It's entirely up to you, Winnie. The hour is late and I must work in my room before I rest. So I bid you goodnight. If you decide to stay, I'll be getting up at dusk tomorrow evening. Do as you please until then, but do not disturb me, whatever the reason." He then turned in the doorway and disappeared into the shadows, which were cast along the landing.

Winnie stood looking at the empty space where he had been. After several moments, she went to the door and shut it tight. There was no lock, she noticed. Taking a chair, Winnie wedged it against the door. She knew that it wouldn't keep anyone out, but the movement of it would wake her. It was better than sleeping with one eye open like she had on so many nights beneath the Embankment.

Winnie went to the bed, lay on it, and spent her first restless night in Thaddeus's house.

Chapter Six

Winnie awoke at a little past nine to the sound of heavy rain beating against her bedroom window. A strong wind nagged and tore about the eaves with an icy fury. She laid spread across the bed, fully dressed. She hadn't felt secure or comfortable enough last night to strip herself bare and climb between the sheets. She had felt vulnerable in the dark, and a certain distrust for Thaddeus still remained. He had been right. The house, the bedroom, the new clothes, the chance to escape her life on the streets, and Thaddeus himself, all seemed too good to be true. She had spent her life distrusting people, because most had hurt her, or let her down in some way. The distrust she felt for her new surroundings and Thaddeus didn't surprise her.

She pulled herself up onto her elbows and gazed sleepily about her new room. It truly was beautiful with its apple white walls and lavish furnishings. It was the kind of room that she had only dared to dream about as a child, as she lay at night and tried to escape the drab surroundings of the care homes she was passed around. Winnie really didn't know what to make of Thaddeus, but so far, he had been nothing but generous, kind, and true to his word. If she left, what did she have to go back to? She had no money, no clothes, or a place to live. Who would employ her? She had been on that merry-go-round before. No one would give you a job if you didn't have a bank account. You couldn't get a bank account without an address, and around and around it went. If she stayed, saved the money that Thaddeus had promised to pay her, then perhaps she could afford to start a new life for herself. She could at last break that vicious circle which she had been trapped in for so many years.

Winnie swung her legs over the side of the bed. She pulled off her boots and wiggled her feet. Standing beside the bed, she let the soft carpet seep between her toes. Winnie headed for the bathroom, undoing the blood-stained top she still wore. She let it slide smoothly off her arms where it fluttered to the floor. Standing naked beside the sunken bath in just her panties, she bent over and loosened the taps. A torrent of hot water cascaded over the shining enamel of the bath. Winnie stepped out of her panties, then climbed into the bath and let the water rise about her. She stopped the flow of water nearly at brimming point and lay back in its warmth. The water soothed her body and she relished the feel of it against her skin. She had forgotten how long it had been since she had had a proper bath or shaved her legs. The strip washes she had managed to have in public bathrooms was nothing compared to this. Even though she had only washed her hair the night before at the station, she needed to wash it again. Winnie needed to wash every part of her past life from her hair, skin, from beneath her fingernails, and between her toes. Taking a nailbrush from the side of the bath, she covered it in soap and raked it up and down her arms, over the flat of her stomach, and down her thighs, until her skin glowed an angry red. She then shaved her legs and armpits.

The water had almost turned cold before she finally reached up for one of the pure white towels, which hung from the rail beside the bath. Standing, she hugged the towel about her frame and slowly began to dry herself. She fixed her hair, and with a new toothbrush she found in one of the bathroom cupboards, she brushed her teeth. It felt so good, that she brushed them twice. Once she was ready, Winnie stepped gingerly from her room at about eleven, dressed in one of the violet tops and short, neat black skirts that Thaddeus had chosen for her. She had pulled her hair back and fastened it in place with a black scarf she had found in one of the many drawers in her room. In fact, the closets and drawers had all been filled to the brim with expensive dresses, trousers, tops, skirts, shoes, hats, handbags, coats, and lingerie, but she had feared to touch any of these without the permission of Thaddeus. After all, she thought, they could've belonged to his dead wife.

She slipped down the lengthy landing, passing closed doors on either side of her. Winnie figured that Thaddeus must be sleeping behind one of them, and not knowing which one, she dared not to enter any of them. He had asked her not to disturb him for any reason. After tiptoeing down the wide staircase, Winnie found herself once again in the vast hall she had stood in the night before. The light was better now, and she crossed to the portraits which hung on the walls. The wall before her was decorated with oil paintings of men. She couldn't be sure, but they appeared to be very old, if not hundreds of years old. The last picture hanging from the wall didn't look so dated. It was a beautifully crafted painting of Thaddeus himself. He stared out of the picture with its silver frame. His dark eyes, scruffy dark hair enclosing his pale face, and his broad mouth set in a nonchalant pose reminded Winnie of how strangely attractive Thaddeus was. He wasn't the typical good-looking guy, but there was something about him, she thought. Something different, but she hadn't quite figured out what.

Winnie passed back along the row, and two things puzzled her. None of the paintings had been signed by the artists, and the men in each painting bore a striking resemblance to Thaddeus himself. Their faces had subtle differences in shape, their hair fashioned in different styles to suit the particular period in time, but all of them had those dark, powerful eyes. Studying the paintings, Winnie decided that they must be his ancestors. She turned on the balls of her feet and crossed to the paintings hanging on the opposite wall. These were paintings of women. Again, all of which appeared to be extremely old. As in the male portraits, the women all bore a striking resemblance to each other. All had a fountain of fiery auburn hair, pale skin, the softest of pink mouths, and green eyes that shone out of the paintings like blazing emeralds. Again, these hadn't been signed.

Winnie crossed to the centre of the hall and looked from one set of paintings to the other. As she passed between them, she noticed that they sat exactly opposite each other, so that their eyes were locked on one another's. She stood in the vast hall, looking up at the paintings. Then when her neck began to ache, she clasped the handle of one of the doors which led from the hallway and eased it open. Peering around the edge of the door, she stepped inside. Winnie found herself in a large dining room. Hazy subdued light spilled in through tall bay windows that stood at the far end of the room and lightened her surroundings. There was a long mahogany table which could have seated at least twenty people comfortably down each side. Bookcases lined the remaining walls from floor to ceiling, with a ladder on wheels propped against the shelves at the far end. She noticed that each book was leather-bound in blues, greens, and deep reds. Their spines were adorned with impressive gold binding, as were the edges of the pages. Winnie closed the door behind her and crossed the hall to the door set into the opposite wall. She pushed it open and stepped into the lounge.

There was another bay window spilling more grey light into the room. Dust moats danced in the slices of grey light. The rain continued to hurl itself against the windows and she wrapped her arms about her shoulders, shivering, and glad to be in the warmth. Squat, leather-backed armchairs and two-seater sofas furnished the room. There was an open fireplace, and Winnie could only imagine how beautiful it would look ablaze on a cold winter's night. In the far corner was the biggest television set she had ever seen, and she went over and switched it on. Sinking down into one of the luxuriant sofas, the TV screen flickered to life.

The midday news was just beginning, and she was surprised that it had gotten so late. She sat before the television more bemused by its size than the World events that were being read by the newscaster. The first story was about the failing economy, and how many more months the country was going to be in a double-dip recession. Winnie had never before concerned herself with such troubles, the life she had led on the streets of London were where her own survival had been her main concern. The second story did grab her attention, as the newsreader began to recount the details of the brutal murder of a student in London. The body had been found in a bedsit, not too far from King's Cross Railway Station. She remembered too well the bitter nights she had spent huddled up there, begging for money so that she could buy food. Winnie listened to how the police were appealing for witnesses. The story cut to a police press conference, where a balding police officer sat behind a large table crammed with microphones. The shoulders of his smart black tunic were covered in crowns, Winnie noticed. He didn't look like the average copper who would hassle her to move on or arrest her for begging; he looked way more important than that.

The police officer had a stern look on his face, and Winnie thought he looked uncomfortable sitting in front of the press before him. As he started to make his statement, Winnie understood why he looked so gaunt and stressed. He started by explaining that he had over twenty-five years of service within the police, but never in that time had he come across such a vicious and horrific crime.

"What is the victim's name?" one of the reporters shouted off-camera.

"That is information I need to withhold at this time, until we have confirmed the identity of the victim."

"So you still don't know who the victim is?" another reporter asked.

"We believe it is the woman who rented that particular room, but we don't want to commit to anything until we have carried out DNA tests on members of the victim's family, to confirm or deny if it is indeed the woman who rented the room."

"The murder took place two nights ago," another reporter reminded him. "How is it you are still yet to identify the victim?"

The police officer, in his neatly-pressed tunic and blazing crowns on his shoulders, looked sombrely at the reporters. He took a moment as if preparing himself for what he had to say next. When he was ready, he said, "The attack was so ferocious that it has as of yet, not been possible to properly identify the victim," the officer explained.

A buzz of excitement swept over the news-hungry reporters, the TV flickered with white light as a burst of cameras all went off at the same time. The officer blinked in the sudden glare of flashing lights.

"So what are the injuries?" a reporter asked.

The officer sat quietly for a moment, his Adam's apple rising slowly in his throat as he swallowed. Then looking at the reporters gathered before him, he said, "It would appear that the perpetrator performed cannibalism on the victim. Either that, or the deceased was attacked by a pack of wild animals."

Hearing this, the horde of photographers and reporters couldn't contain themselves any longer as they hailed a wave of questions at the now-dazed officer. Winnie lent forward and snapped off the television. She didn't want to hear about what was going on in London. She was away from that place now and didn't want to be reminded of it. More than that - she didn't ever want to go back. Maybe she had done the right thing by coming down to Cornwall with Thaddeus. It couldn't be any more dangerous than the risks she had taken to survive over the last few years. As she sat and wondered on the life she had led, and how she had never known what dangers each day might have brought, Winnie slowly gazed up where Thaddeus now slept in one of the rooms above her. As her thoughts turned to the man who had offered her a new start, she knew in her heart that she had taken another big risk.

Chapter Seven

Scaring herself with the news bulletin, and filling her head with paranoid thoughts about Thaddeus's motives for bringing her to his secluded home on the coast, Winnie knew she had to break the destructive train of thoughts which were now gnawing away inside of her. If she didn't stop listening to them - shut them out - she would go mad for sure. So switching the TV back on, she sat for the next hour and watched Sesame Street, trying to unburden her troubled mind with the company of Big Bird, Bert, and Ernie, Elmo, and the Cookie Monster. It wasn't a programme she had watched since being very small, and she enjoyed feeling like a little kid again.

By the end of the show she had counted to ten with the Count and discovered the letter 'E'. Winnie was in a much brighter mood. As the end credits rolled, she switched off the TV again, and passed through the lounge to the kitchen. It was huge, and like most of the other rooms in the house, it was furnished with all the modern appliances which were assured to make your life easier. A wooden table sat in the centre of the room surrounded by four chairs. Winnie crossed to it and found fifty pounds. Under the money, Winnie discovered a note. Scribbled across it were the words, *Buy something nice for dinner - Thad.*

Winnie had spent the rest of the day preparing Thaddeus's and her own evening meal. She had found little in the cupboards or freezer, so after cladding herself in a waterproof coat she had found hanging on the back of the kitchen door, she ventured out of the house in search of some shops. On her journey down from the house, she discovered that it occupied land which led down to a jagged-looking coastline and the sea. Looking out over the edge of the cliffs, with icy rain driving into her face, Winnie knew she had been correct the night before. The house was set high on a hill, surrounded by a dense crop of trees. As she looked out at the waves which crashed against the cliffs, she could see St. Ives stretched out before her and the continuing rugged coastline. Although the new world she found herself in was bleak and cold, she couldn't help but see its beauty. With the wind nagging at her hair, and rain running the length of her face like tears, Winnie followed the narrow coastal path below. In town, she came across a small supermarket. With some of the money Thaddeus had left on the table, she bought their dinner and made her way back up the hill to the house.

Winnie stood in the kitchen as the night soaked up the remainder of the day. She laid two places at the kitchen table, a knife, fork, and a spoon for each of them. A vase stood in the centre of the table filled with heather, which she had gathered on her return journey from the store. The meal was cooked and warming under the grill. Pleased with herself, she waited for Thaddeus to wake.

Her wait wasn't a long one as she heard movement from above, then the sound of his footfalls on the stairs. For the first time since arriving at the house, Winnie began to feel nervous. Not of the man himself, but of the little things. Like would they find enough to talk about, and were there going to be any of those agonising drawn-out silences? What would he be like to work for? Would he be an arsehole? She wondered.

As she heard him approach, she pulled the scarf from her hair, and with a quick flick of her head, sent her auburn hair cascading over her shoulders like liquid copper. She smartened her top and straightened her trousers with the palms of her hands. Winnie stood before the table as Thaddeus entered. He stood in the doorway, his hair more of a mess than she remembered. His eyes shone brilliantly like two glowing coals in his pale face. He wore a white shirt which was open at the throat, revealing just the brief glimpse of his chest. His legs were hidden beneath a pair of faded blue denims, and he wore loafers on his feet. Out of his suit, he looked younger - relaxed somehow.

Thaddeus smiled and said, "Good evening, Winnie."

Smiling back, Winnie gestured to a seat. "I've cooked your dinner, Thaddeus." It had been a long time since anyone had trusted her with any kind of responsibility. Okay, so she had only chosen the meal, cooked it, and prepared the table. To most, these were just a series of menial and mundane tasks, but it had given her a sense of self-worth and a glimmer of purpose. It had been a long time since she had felt either of those things.

Thaddeus eyed the table curiously as he took his seat. Winnie turned to the grill, and covering her hands with a towel, she plucked two plates out and placed them on the table. She took her seat. Winnie looked across at Thaddeus, who sat staring down at the plate of fish fingers, oven-ready chips, and a mound of baked beans.

"Is everything okay?" she asked.

"I hadn't realised I had employed you for your sense of humour," he said, not once taking his eyes off the meal before him.

"I'm not sure what you mean?" Winnie said.

Ignoring her question, he prodded one of the fish fingers with his slender fingers. "What is this?"

Winnie remained silent, her own knife and fork poised over her plate of food. "I don't know what you mean, Thad....."

"Are you trying to be funny?" he asked, cutting over her and fixing her with a dark stare.

Winnie felt flustered. "No, Thaddeus, it's your dinner. I cooked it for you. Is there something wrong?"

He scoffed a cynical laugh and pushed the plate back towards her. "I'd say there was something wrong, wouldn't you?"

Seeing the rejection of her meal and all her hard work, she, too became annoyed. "I'm not sure I follow."

"This isn't a meal," he sneered.

"It looks like food to me," she shot back.

"Surely you don't expect me to eat this?" he said, looking down at the food again. "This isn't food."

"It is where I come from," Winnie said, trying to hide her growing anger. Then pushing her chair back from the table, she stood up. With tears burning in the corners of her eyes and feeling useless, she looked at Thaddeus and said, "When you're freezing cold, tired, and starving hungry, you would eat anything. I guess you wouldn't have the faintest idea how that would feel. I know people back in London who would sell themselves for a meal like that tonight."

Thaddeus looked at her, his face impassive and said, "I'm sorry; perhaps we should Fed-Ex it to them."

Drawing a deep breath, Winnie clenched her hands into fists by her sides. She couldn't believe what she had just heard him say. With silent tears now streaming down her face, she looked at Thaddeus and said, "You prick."

Without waiting for him to reply, Winnie raced across the kitchen to the door. As if realising how much he had hurt her feelings, he dropped his head in shame. "I'm sorry. I didn't mean that. Please forgive me."

"Screw you!" Winnie hissed, yanking open the door.

But before she even knew what was happening, Thaddeus was beside her, his hand gently falling upon her arm.

"I'm truly sorry," he whispered.

"Fuck off!" she blurted out through her tears. Thaddeus removed his hand but stayed standing beside her. Then leaning in close to her, he whispered in her ear.

"I'm sorry, Winnie. It was thoughtless of me. Please forgive me."

Covering her face with her hands, Winnie bent forward and began to sob. His apology seemed to have sent her into a new flood of tears.

Then reaching out, Thaddeus placed a hand lightly on her shoulder.

"Shhh, Winnie," he soothed, "I'm sorry, I never meant to make you cry."

She continued to sob, and through her tears she began to speak.

"Not...not your fault...I'm a thick...bitch...." Winnie sobbed. Perhaps she was thick? She wondered. After all, he wasn't paying her two hundred pounds a week to cook fish fingers. Why had Thaddeus found it necessary to be so cruel, though?

He removed his hand from her shoulder. It felt odd being so close to her. To be standing so close to Winnie was like betraying his wife in some way. The smell of Winnie's hair and skin stirred feelings in him. It reminded him of what his wife had once smelt like, and he wished now that he had got Winnie a different shampoo. It had been a mistake to buy the same one. However much he wanted to stand next to Winnie and convince her he was sorry for hurting her feelings, Thaddeus had to walk away.

"You're not thick, Winnie. You did your best under the circumstances. I should have realised that and been more understanding and less fussy. It won't happen again," Thaddeus said, going back to the table.

Winnie drew her head up. A thin line of snot trailed from her right nostril and she cuffed it away with her sleeve. She realised what she had done and knew that old habits were the hardest to break. She wasn't on the street anymore. It was more than that. Thaddeus had shown a flicker of cruelness she hadn't expected. What had she expected? She didn't know him. She knew nothing about him. Only what he had cared to tell her.

Staring at him, she spoke softly without any malice in her voice and said, "I know it won't happen again, Thaddeus, because I'm leaving. You don't need a stupid tramp like me hanging around, cluttering up your beautiful home and cooking you naff meals."

Thaddeus looked at her, and for the second time since she had met him, Winnie saw desperation in his eyes.

"Please don't leave, Winnie. We can work things out. Don't go back to London. It isn't safe for you there. You can stay here. I'll teach you to cook. We'll be good for each other."

Winnie looked upon his face. She felt confused. "What's the point of employing me to cook and clean for you if you're going to cook all the meals yourself?"

"I didn't say I was going to cook all the meals - I said I would teach you," he tried to smile, but that look of desperation still darkened his eyes.

"But what do you get from this deal?" Winnie asked with a shake of her head.

"Like I said in London, Winnie, you take care of my home and put up with my eccentric ways, and I'll give you a home, a wage," he said. "I'll even teach you to cook."

She began to dry her eyes and said, "It seems a little strange to me, Thaddeus."

"What's so strange about it?" he asked with a shrug of his shoulders. "We're both a little strange if you think about it. We can make a good team. You've got nothing to go back to, and I've got nothing up here all on my own. What do you say?"

Winnie stared at him for a long moment. Half of her felt unsure of him, but there was another part of him that fascinated her, and she didn't know why. If he had wanted to have harmed her in some way - wouldn't he have done it by now? Okay, so he was pissed off with the whole fish finger thing, but she could tell by the size of the house, the material wealth, he was used to finer things. Maybe it was just one of his eccentricities he had warned her about. Besides, what was there to go back to? Getting into an argument about her cooking skills was nothing compared to what she had left behind. She knew in her heart that Ruby Little wouldn't have thrown away the chance, if she had been offered it.

Finally, she whispered, "Okay, I'll stay."

"Thank you," Thaddeus whispered and turned away.

He scraped their uneaten meals into the trash. Placing their empty plates into the dishwasher, he looked back at her and said, "Get a coat. I'm going to take you out for dinner."

Winnie was just about to leave the room, when Thaddeus said, "Wear the grey coat with the hood."

Looking back at him, she cocked an eyebrow and said, "Why that particular coat?"

"It has a hood," he said right back. "It's raining. Besides, I like the coat."

As she left the kitchen, he plucked a waterproof coat from the hook on the back of the door. Flicking off the kitchen light, he made his way to the front door. He took the silver cigarette case from his trouser pocket and smoked while he waited for Winnie. She hadn't been gone long when he heard her footfalls on the stairs. Thaddeus looked back to see Winnie step off the bottom stair and into the huge hall. The long, grey coat swished just above her ankles. She almost seemed to float towards Thaddeus who stood by the front door, the cigarette dangling from the corner of his mouth. As she came towards him, Thaddeus noticed that she had daubed the faintest hint of green eye shadow above her eyes, a smudge of blusher on each cheek, and a deep, red lipstick now coated her soft lips.

He could hardly mask his smile as she stopped before him. "You look stunning," he breathed.

She let out a little laugh of embarrassment and blushed. "I found the makeup on the dressing table in my room," she said. "It's okay to use it, isn't it?"

"Use whatever you like," he smiled, and pulled the hood of her coat up so it covered the back of her head and the sides of her face.

"Whose is it?" she asked.

"It's yours," he said, hooking a long length of her hair out from beneath her hood so it hung against the right side of her face. "Perfect," he whispered, looking at her.

"Perfect for what?" she smiled.

"For dinner," he winked back and led her out into the night.

Chapter Eight

The small coastal town of St. Ives was quiet during the winter months. There weren't any tourists and they wouldn't arrive until Easter, when all the little tea shops, ice cream parlours, and shell shops would open, eagerly awaiting the rush. Tonight was cold, and the rain drove into them as they walked huddled together down the meandering cobbled streets to the harbour. The smell of the sea was strong as it wafted on the wind and salted their lips. Boat rigging whipped vigorously against the masts of the boats moored in the harbour.

They came across the restaurant that Thaddeus had eaten in twice before since coming to live in the town. It was aptly named the *Light House*. On entering, their wet coats were taken from them, and they were ushered to a quiet table for two at the rear of the eating area. Thaddeus requested that Winnie be seated with her back to the restaurant window, which looked out onto the harbour. Their cutlery and wine glasses twinkled with a warm orange brilliance from an open fire that roared and spat a few feet from them. Thaddeus ordered a bottle of white wine, while Winnie gazed in awe about the restaurant.

"What are you having, Thaddeus?" she asked over the sound of the snapping wood in the hearth.

He rested his hands beneath his chin and spoke, "You were cooking dinner tonight, so you can choose."

She looked down at the menu and said, "I wouldn't know where to start. You choose."

He grinned at her across the table. "Let me see," he said reading the menu.

Before long, the waiter had arrived beside them.

"We would like two avocados for starters and for our main course, chicken stuffed with mushrooms, a side order of roast beef, and a mixture of vegetables."

Thaddeus looked up at the ruddy-faced waiter and smiled. "Thank you."

"Very good, sir," the waiter nodded and disappeared into the kitchen.

"Better than those fish fingers, huh?" Winnie smiled at him.

But it was as if Thaddeus hadn't heard her. He was suddenly staring over her right shoulder and out of the window and onto the street outside. It was as if someone or something had grabbed his attention.

"Is everything okay?" Winnie asked.

As if being snapped out of a dream, he looked at Winnie and said, "Everything is just fine."

"What were you looking at?" she quizzed him.

"It was nothing," he said back.

Thaddeus sat and watched the burning embers of the fire cast their golden reflections in her copper hair. The silky curls looked as if they were alight. Then a sudden urge came over him to reach out and lose his hands in its soft texture, to soak up its seething light through his fingertips. He stifled the temptation and spoke to her.

"So if you don't mind me asking, where is your family? Do you have any brothers or sisters?"

She looked squarely at him. "I've never known my father. He did a bunk before I was even born. My mum was only sixteen herself when she fell pregnant with me. I guess that's why she gave me up."

"Gave you up?" Thaddeus asked. "Adoption, you mean?"

Winnie could sense what she believed to be genuine concern in his voice for her.

"My mother had an older sister and she dumped me on her when I was barely two years old," Winnie explained. "But my auntie didn't really want me. She had three kids of her own. Her husband was hardly ever around. So she kicked me out into the care of the local authorities. I was bounced from one family to the next. Missed lots of school and stuff like that. When I was thirteen, I ended up living with this family called the Martins. The dad was a real pig, he made me unhappy. So I ran away when I was fourteen. Got picked up a few times by the cops and ended up back in care, but I never hung around for long. In the end, the cops stopped looking for me. They had more important stuff to deal with, right?"

The waiter reappeared and opened the bottle of wine. Thaddeus seemed annoyed by the interruption. The waiter poured half a glass for Thaddeus.

"Would you like to taste, sir?"

Thaddeus kept his eye on Winnie and just waved his hand at the waiter, who acknowledged this by saying, "Very good, sir." He poured a glass for Winnie, placed the bottle on the table, and left.

"Where do you come from?" Thaddeus inquired of her.

"All over the place," she half-smiled. Then looking up at Thaddeus, she said, "I haven't always been homeless since running away."

"How come?" Thaddeus asked, taking a sip of wine.

"When I was about fifteen, I was with this guy called Simon. He was older than me - not by much - but enough. Old enough for the council to pay his rent, so he had his own place. He was really good to me at first. You know, like real thoughtful and understanding," she said. "I stopped wanting to run away because he made me feel special inside. For the first time, I felt needed."

"What went wrong?" Thaddeus asked, now regretting how he had patronised Winnie earlier that evening.

"I guess he knew how much I needed him and he kinda took advantage of the fact," Winnie explained. "I think he got to thinking that he could treat me however he wanted, because I needed him so much. You know, he thought because I didn't have much else going for me, I'd let him get away with whatever he wanted."

"Did he mistreat you?"

"No, not really," she said, and briefly looked away.

In that moment Thaddeus knew that this Simon had hurt her and probably badly, but he didn't want to push her into telling him something that she was uncomfortable talking about.

"He never laid a finger on me," Winnie insisted as if being able to read Thaddeus's thoughts. "He knew I was insecure, and he played on that. To tell you the truth, Thaddeus, I would have preferred a good thump. At least you know where you stand, but when you've got someone playing with your heart all the time, boosting you up one minute and knocking you down the next, you never know where you stand. Believe me, that hurt a lot more than a good thump."

Thaddeus sipped at his wine as the waiter reappeared and placed their starter before them. The waiter was gone as quickly as he had arrived. Thaddeus and Winnie tucked into their avocados.

"How did he knock you down then?" he pushed ever so carefully.

"Bit by bit, he ate away at my confidence by sleeping with other women. He would tell me about them - how much better they were than me. He wanted me to try stuff that I wasn't comfortable with. My confidence got more and more knocked, and each day I continued to stay with him, I felt that little bit less special."

Thaddeus pushed his empty plate away and took to his wine again. Winnie continued to eat.

"So what did you do about this Simon?" he asked her.

Winnie chewed over her last mouthful, and then continued her story. "I did what I know best, and ran. I went back to London. At first I kidded myself that I would only stay a day or two. I fooled myself into believing that I would find work somehow. One day leads into another, then into weeks and months. You get dirtier; the tiredness drains you along with the hunger and the sleepless nights. Then the despair sets in. You end up staying - you become trapped."

Their empty starter plates were whisked away and their main course was laid before them. Curls of steam rose up off the chicken's golden and crisp meat, and the beef looked almost raw as it sat in a pool of its own juices, red with blood. The vegetables were in a side dish and they looked soft and bright in colour. Thaddeus picked up a large knife and began to cut away at the chicken. The knife slipped through its succulent body as easily as cutting butter. He laid several thick slices on Winnie's plate, as she in turn heaped a spoonful of vegetables onto Thaddeus's plate and then her own. Thaddeus helped himself to a large portion of the chicken, tearing both its legs off and placing them on his plate alongside a thick slice of the bloody beef. They both sat and forked the food into their mouths.

Thaddeus watched her while she ate, and something she had said played over and over in his mind. Winnie had said that what she did best was run - that's all she knew what to do. She had run from her aunt, run from the care homes, run from Simon to London, and had now run away from there to be with him. Winnie never seemed to hang around for too long and he knew that he would need her to stay a while longer - a lot longer. Thaddeus found himself captivated by her energy, her anger, the fire that seemed to burn brightly inside of her. She was alive and she wasn't stupid. He hadn't expected that - but he liked it. Those feelings he would have to bury somewhere deep inside. He couldn't afford to let himself care about her.

Winnie looked at Thaddeus, the crossed words they'd had back at the house now seemed like a far-off memory. Nobody had ever bothered to sit and listen to her before. Nobody had ever cared enough. Thaddeus was already on his second helping of chicken when he noticed Winnie watching him over the rim of her glass as she sipped her wine. "What about you, Thaddeus?"

He looked straight at her as he refilled her glass again and said, "What about me?"

"Tell me about your life," she said.

He turned and looked into the fire. His voice was soft, almost a whisper. "I wouldn't know where to start, Winnie."

The world swam lazily back and forth as the wine relaxed her and strengthened her confidence. "How about at the beginning," she said.

Thaddeus looked away from the fire and back at Winnie. "The beginning," he said thoughtfully. "Life is full of beginnings and endings. I wouldn't know which one too chose."

"Start from the day you met your wife," Winnie found the confidence to ask him. "You said you knew you loved her from the very first moment you saw her. I'd like to hear about that. It sounds romantic."

Again, Thaddeus looked away and said, "I'd rather not talk about that. I still find the death of my wife hard to come to terms with."

"I'm sorry," Winnie whispered. "I didn't mean to..."

"Let's go home," he said, suddenly standing. "It's getting late and I have work to do."

He held out his hand and Winnie took hold of it. She swayed slightly and Thaddeus steadied her. The wine had clouded her mind, and Winnie failed to notice that there wasn't any cut on Thaddeus's hand. If she had noticed this, Winnie might have wondered where the blood had come from, the blood which had stained her top on the train as she ran away with Thaddeus to his home in Cornwall.

Chapter Nine

The rain had started to ease a little, but it was cold, and Winnie pulled her coat tight about herself. With the hood pulled over her head, she peered beneath it and up at the night sky, which was heavy with clouds. The cold night air did little to clear the fog in her mind and she wished now that she had drunk just a little less wine. Thaddeus walked beside her, and every time she stumbled or lost her footing on the uneven dirt road which led up the hill, he would gently take her arm.

Cold and wet, Winnie glanced at him and said, "Don't you have a car, Thaddeus?"

"Why, can you drive?" he asked her.

"No," she mumbled.

"Neither can I," he smiled back. "I've never had the need for a car."

"Oh," she said thoughtfully, but her head felt too woozy to think about it very much.

They walked in silence until they reached the gate in the wall that surrounded Thaddeus's huge home. They cut through the crop of trees, the sound of rain drumming against the leaves overhead. Stepping out from amongst the trees, a single shaft of bluey-white moonlight had broken through the clouds and made a pool of light on the ground before the house. Winnie looked up and could see a half moon peering around the edge of a bank of clouds.

"Isn't it beautiful?" she heard Thaddeus whisper.

"Yes," she breathed, the rain spattering her upturned face.

"The moonlight makes you look very beautiful," Thaddeus suddenly said.

"Aw, you're just saying that," Winnie giggled, looking at him. There was a part of her that so much wanted what he said to be true. She had never been told that before by anyone. Although it made her feel slightly uneasy coming from a man she hardly knew, she liked hearing those words. She liked the way he was looking at her.

Reaching out with his hand, Thaddeus brushed the damp lengths of hair from her cheeks, as if wanting to see more of her face. In the moonlight she truly did look beautiful, he thought, and he tried to push those feelings away. The moonlight made her look like china, fragile and breakable.

"What's wrong?" Winnie asked, slowly pulling his hand away from her face. Even through the fogginess of her mind, she could see that his look of wonder at her had changed to one of sadness - remorse.

"Wait here," he said, turning and heading towards the house.

"Where are you going?" she called out, now standing alone in the shaft of blue moonlight.

"I'm going to get my camera," he called out as he fumbled for his door keys in his coat pocket. "I want to take a photo of you."

"But it's raining!" she gasped, not knowing whether she should be flattered by his behaviour or not. She couldn't remember the last time anyone had ever wanted to take a picture of her. "Can't it wait until tomorrow?"

But Thaddeus had gone, disappearing inside the house.

Winnie stood alone in the moonlight and rain. Although she was kind of pleased that Thaddeus wanted to take a picture of her, she hoped he would hurry up. She felt cold and wet through. Not only that, she felt ridiculous standing alone, with her hood up, her hair all bedraggled and plastered to the sides of her face. Winnie doubted that she looked very beautiful at all. With her self-esteem at its usual low, she wondered if perhaps he wasn't taking the piss - having a laugh at her expense.

So wanting to make sure that she looked her best, she positioned herself so she could see her reflection in one of the tall bay windows set into the front of the house.

With her fingers almost numb with cold, she combed them through the wispy lengths of hair that hung limply against her cheeks. She turned quickly sideways, then front again, checking out her profile. The wind suddenly picked up, blowing a flurry of leaves from beneath the trees behind her.

There was a snapping noise, like feet treading over fallen twigs. Winnie spun around and peered into the slices of darkness between the black and knotted tree trunks. The sound came again.

"Hello?" she gasped. "Is there anyone there?"

The noise stopped, or was it drowned out by another sudden gust of wind? A shower of sodden leaves scattered into the air again, and then settled as the wind dropped. Winnie peered into the darkness once more, then turned back to face the window, and then screamed.

Reflected back in the window, she could see three pale faces looming out of the darkness behind her. With her heart in her throat, she turned again, but the faces were now gone. Her heart raced so fast and loud, she could hear it beating in her ears. The wind suddenly howled all around her, blowing her hair out from beneath her hood and covering her face. She closed her eyes against the wind, her hair, and the driving rain, and in that moment of darkness, she heard voices.

Snapping open her eyes again, and clawing her hair from her face, the wind wrapped itself around Winnie like a cold, wet blanket and almost seemed to whisper in her ears.

*Come home...*the wind cried as it circled her.

*Come home...he will kill you...just like the others...*the wind whispered.

Winnie threw her hands over her ears, closing her eyes against the leaves that now whipped violently around her as if she were trapped in a raging storm. Then, she felt her hands being pulled free from over her ears.

"Winnie!" a voice shouted.

This time it wasn't a voice carried on the wind that she heard. Opening her eyes, Winnie stared into Thaddeus's pale face.

"Winnie!" he shouted, taking her by the shoulders and gently shaking her as if waking her from a dream.

"There were faces," she breathed, then glanced back over her shoulder at the treeline.

"Faces?" Thaddeus asked. "What faces? Where?"

"They were staring out of the woods at me," she murmured, feeling confused and disorientated. "There were voices, too."

"Voices?" Thaddeus said, sounding evermore confused.

"It was like they were talking to me," she said, and her lower lip trembled as she stared into the darkness that separated the trees.

"I didn't hear anything," Thaddeus said, and seeing that she was trembling, he pulled her close.

"You were inside," she tried to explain. "You wouldn't have heard them because of the wind."

"Where were these faces?" Thaddeus quizzed her.

"I'm not sure," she said, a deep frown forming across her brow. "I saw them reflected in the window."

"Reflected in the window," he frowned back at her. Then a half-smile tugged at the corners of his mouth. "Are you sure it wasn't just the moonlight distorting your own reflection back at you?"

"No, I'm sure," Winnie whispered, now starting to feel confused, a sense of self-doubt taking hold of her. "What about the voices?"

"The wind perhaps?" he said, looking at her. "We're high up here. The wind can sound like a million different things as it cuts across the fields and rages against the cliff faces."

"Really?" Winnie asked him, a part of her hoping that what he said was true.

"Sure it does," he said. "Sometimes, when the wind blows really hard, you couldn't be blamed for mistaking it for a giant pack of wolves racing up the hillside."

"But they sounded so real," she mumbled.

Then, leading her gently out of the shaft of moonlight, the wind and the rain, they headed towards the house. "I think you had a little too much to drink tonight," he told her. "You'll laugh about this in the morning."

They reached the open front door, and looking back at the pool of moonlight, Winnie whispered, "You never took that picture."

"I couldn't find my camera," he smiled back at her, and closed the door.

Chapter Ten

Thaddeus took their wet coats and hung them up to dry in the kitchen. He made them both a cup of sweet black coffee and Winnie sat at the kitchen table. Her head still felt a little groggy as she tried to make sense of what she had really seen outside in the storm. Her cheeks glowed scarlet from where she had been left waiting outside in the cold. Winnie sat and shivered before him, as Thaddeus pushed a mug of coffee towards her.

"Here, drink this. It'll warm you up."

Thaddeus knew that Winnie was still a little tipsy from the wine, but he wanted to give her a list of instructions for tomorrow so that there wouldn't be any more mistakes and embarrassments.

He sat opposite her and said, "Winnie, tomorrow morning, a bundle of foreign newspapers will be delivered. They arrive once a week on a Thursday morning."

She took a sip of her coffee, and then said, "Why do you have foreign newspapers delivered? What's wrong with the English ones?"

Thaddeus smiled. "I have English newspapers delivered as well, but I like to keep abreast of what's happening all over the world."

Winnie started to relax a little now that she was in the warmth beneath the glow of the kitchen lighting, the feelings of fear she had felt outside were now slowly ebbing away, like the broken pieces of a nightmare at dawn. With the mug of coffee warming her hands, Winnie looked with surprise across the table at Thaddeus and said, "You mean you can read and understand loads of different languages? What countries do these newspapers come from?"

Thaddeus found her disbelief and wonderment a little amusing. "Yes, I can speak many different languages. The papers I have delivered are mainly European, but I also have papers from America, Australia, Japan, China, and a few more besides."

Winnie sat up in her seat, eyes wide with interest. "You can speak and read in Japanese?"

"Yes," he smiled.

"I don't believe it!"

"Winnie, would I lie to you?" and his eyes twinkled.

"Go on then, prove it. Say something in Japanese," she egged him on.

He laughed a little again and met her gaze. "You embarrass me, Winnie; not now, maybe another time. Let us master the English language first, and then I will teach you another."

Winnie frowned, but she didn't want to press the issue. She would have loved to have heard him say just a few words in another language, to hear his soft voice in another tongue. Then looking at him, she said, "So what's wrong with my English?"

"Nothing," he said. "But I remember you telling me while you ate pasta the other night, that your reading and writing wasn't great."

"I was hardly at school," she said, trying to excuse herself.

"No matter," Thaddeus said. "That was in the past. This is a new beginning. I have plenty of books. I'm sure I'll be able to find one that you'll enjoy reading." Then, changing the subject, he said, "When the papers come, just take them in for me and leave them in the hallway. Could you also give the place a bit of a clean? I haven't touched it in over a week."

Winnie nodded and said, "Sure."

"As for shopping, buy meats: pork, lamb, steak, and liver. Get some fresh vegetables, bread, milk, fruit, and whatever else you fancy."

"But what do you want me to cook?"

"Nothing," he said with a shake of his head. "I'm going to teach you to cook, remember? When I wake tomorrow evening, we shall cook together. You just get the food."

Winnie finished her coffee, and now just wanting to get some sleep, she said, "Okay, anything else?"

"Yes, the clothes in your bedroom – treat them as your own. Wear whatever you want, when you want. They used to be my wife's."

"Oh, I couldn't. I wouldn't feel...." Winnie started to protest.

"She wouldn't have minded. I know she would have wanted you to have them."

"But..." Winnie started up again.

Before she had the chance to finish what it was she had wanted to say, Thaddeus got up from his seat and said, "She really wouldn't have minded."

He crossed to the kitchen door, paused, and turned to face her, "Thank you for a wonderful evening, Winnie, your company has been enchanting. I shall see you tomorrow."

He turned to go through the door as Winnie called after him, "What was her name?"

Thaddeus stopped in midstride. He paused for what seemed an eternity, and then turned to face her.

"Frances," he said, looking down at the floor.

"What did she look like?" Winnie dared to ask, remembering how he had avoided the subject earlier that evening.

Slowly, Thaddeus raised his head and fixed her sleepy eyes with his own cool, dark stare, then answered her question. "Strangely enough, Frances looked a lot like you," he said.

He turned on his heels and left the kitchen for his room high above, where, as far as Winnie knew, he stayed until the following evening.

Chapter Eleven

"You are truly beautiful," he whispered in her ear, using one hand to unzip her dress.

"I bet you always say that," the girl giggled at the touch of his breath against her neck.

He made no reply as he slowly pulled the dress down over her shoulders, releasing her ample breasts. Swaying slightly, she helped him pull her dress and panties down over her hips and thighs, where they made a whispering sound against her flesh. He guided her away from the discarded clothing, and looked at her in the moonlight; it seemed to slice her living room in two.

"So beautiful," he said, looking at her.

"You'll have to be quiet, or you'll wake the baby," she giggled again, pointing upwards.

Ignoring her, he looked at how her white skin glimmered like marble in the moonlight.

"So much flesh," he mused.

"Hey, you cheeky bastard," she half-smiled, the strong smell of wine on her breath. "What are you saying, that I'm fat?" And she crossed her arms over her breasts.

"No, no," he smiled at her, gently pulling her arms away again. From the moment he had seen her sitting in the corner of the pub, with the wind and the rain roaring outside and the crash of the waves against the quay, he knew she would be the one. Again, it had all been far too easy for him. A few drinks, the right words, and a little harmless flirting. That was all it took. He was beautiful too, he knew that and so did they. Most women and even a few men turned their heads and looked twice when they first saw him. He wasn't interested in them. He liked the girls who wouldn't look at him, who wouldn't match his stare because they believed they weren't worthy. If he were to be honest - they weren't. Not many were.

But they went with him easily, without a fight, because they were needy, lonely, or both. The girl who stood before him was an ideal candidate. As she had knocked back the drinks he had placed before her, she had groaned on and on about how the father of her child had left her, how lonely she was, how unattractive she felt, and on and on and on. He wasn't interested in any of that shit. He was only interested in satisfying the hunger that burnt inside of him. As he sat and drank, the more she talked. Christ, she made her life sound so fucking depressing, he honestly began to wonder if she wouldn't be better off dead after all. She talked about how she only earnt minimum wage at the local store, and it wasn't even enough to pay for childcare. How since she was the only one of her friends who had become a mum, they didn't understand. They didn't want to sit in of a night - they wanted to be out having fun and not wiping a baby's arse. Even the friend she had planned to meet tonight had failed to show up. On and on and on she went. He just sat and smiled, pretending to listen intently, telling her that he couldn't understand why such an attractive young woman was being so hard on herself, though all the while his innards seethed, and his blood felt like it was boiling in his veins as the hunger gnawed away at him.

Then when he thought he couldn't take it anymore, and that he might just rip her fucking throat out in the bar and be done with it, she staggered to her feet, giggling that she hadn't meant to be out so long as she had left her baby asleep in his cot. Then, just like he knew she would, the girl looked down at him and said, "I've got a bottle of wine in the fridge at home, if you fancy another?"

"Sure," he had smiled at her.

She pushed open the front door and stumbled into the hallway, kicking her heels off as she went. He closed the front door behind her, but not tight. He always left the door open just an inch so the others could join him.

Now he took her in his arms and steadied her.

"We can do it on the sofa if you like," she said, as he leant in close and kissed her neck.

He could smell her skin and cheap perfume. Beneath it, he could smell what he had really come for and it pulsed through her veins in a rush. He gripped her left breast with his hand, and she gasped. He could feel her heart thumping just beneath his fist, and his, matched its frantic pace.

"How about on the floor?" she slurred in his ear, taking his hand that still cupped her breast and guided him downwards.

"The floor would be good," he whispered back.

She kicked aside kiddie toys, which cluttered the floor of the living room, and lay on her back. Then kneeling over her, he gripped her wrists and pinned her to the floor.

"It's going to be like that, is it?" she squirmed with a rush of excitement beneath him. Then she froze and peered over his shoulder as she heard a sound in the hallway.

"Stop," she whispered. "I think there is someone else in here."

"Oh, I wouldn't worry about them," he grinned into her face. "They are just my friends."

"What the fuck are you talking about?" she said, looking back up into his face. It wasn't the beautifully good-looking face that had turned her on so much before. Those wonderful brown eyes were now deep black holes, and his full lips were now stretched open across his face, disappearing behind his ears. In the moonlight, which sliced through the window, the girl at first thought he had somehow managed to put on one of those freaky-looking clown masks. As he spoke, his lips rolled back, revealing a set of long, jagged teeth.

"*Get off me!*" she screeched, bucking her hips in an attempt to throw him clear of her. He was too strong and pinned her effortlessly to the floor. Then, with her eyes bulging, she glanced over his shoulder to see two others enter the living room – one male, the other female. At first glance, the girl thought them both to be as beautiful as the man had once been, but as they stepped into the moonlight, she screamed at the sight of their ragged mouths, which looked as if they had split their faces in two.

"*Please don't hurt me,*" she begged softly.

"That's what they all say," the man pinning her to the floor whispered, his lips spreading too wide across his face.

She kicked wildly out with her legs, but just like her arms, her legs became pinned to the floor by the female and male.

"Please..." she struggled against them, as the female holding her leg drew her tongue along the outside of the girl's thigh, as if tasting her.

Then, from above, a different kind of cry cut through the night – the sound of a baby. The girl glanced up at the ceiling and so did the others.

She saw the delight in their sunken black eyes and sobbed, "Please don't hurt my baby. Please...I won't tell..." but the last of her sentence became nothing more than a series of undecipherable gurgles and spluttering's, as the vampire lunged forward and greedily ripped out her throat.

The sound of their ravenous feeding drowned out the sound of the baby's cries for a while, but not for long.

Chapter Twelve

Winnie lay on her bed, arms stretched out on either side of her. She was cold, wearing only a pair of panties and a bra. Her eyes were closed and she didn't need to open them to know that her room was in complete darkness. Her heart raced behind her narrow chest and her mind swam sickly from side to side. She wished again that she hadn't drunk so much. She reached for the covers, then stopped. There was a noise - she was sure of it, like someone moving in her room. She wanted to open her eyes but couldn't. It was like they were being held shut by two invisible thumbs.

Then she felt the cool touch of a hand on her ankle. A man's hand. Strong. Moving like the legs of a giant spider, she could feel fingers slowly traveling up her leg. They worked slowly, caressing her calf muscle, stroking and pressing her inner thigh. She reached out with her hand, to brush it away but there was no one there.

Open your eyes, she cursed herself. She couldn't.

The room fell silent again. The only sound she could hear was her own heart thumping in her ears. She felt scared but didn't want to yell out, in case she disturbed Thaddeus.

Then, she felt those fingers again as they passed over her stomach and worked their way up between her breasts. Winnie reached out again but still couldn't find anybody there.

Open your eyes, the voice inside urged her. She couldn't or wouldn't. She was no longer sure. Then she felt the warm wetness of lips covering her own.

She felt scared now, but kind of excited, too. How was that possible? She wondered behind her closed eyelids. The mouth worked its way up her throat and nicked at her fair skin. She moaned in pain, and then the mouth covered hers again. A tongue darted into her mouth and she kissed back. Then for the first time, she could feel the whole of his body pressing down over hers. Winnie reached out with her hands for him, wanting him now, yet hating him. She could feel no one there.

The mouth broke away from hers and she threw open her eyes and although the room was in complete darkness, his face shone palely down into hers. She looked up at Thaddeus. His eyes bore right into hers and he smiled...

...Winnie sat bolt upright in bed, her whole body covered in a sticky sweat. She sucked frantic mouthfuls of air into her lungs as she fought to breathe. With her heart racing, she peered about her room as the early morning sun streamed through the windows in thin ribbons of light. Her head ached from the alcohol she had drunk the night before. Winnie sat and shivered as the last fragments of her dream ebbed away. She felt troubled by her dream. Not because it had scared her - but it had felt so real. Not just the feel of his touch, but the feelings she had felt while kissing him.

Swinging her legs over the side of the bed, Winnie tried to push the last remaining shards of the dream away, which still lingered on in the furthest corners of her mind. Why had she dreamt of them together like that? She thought, as she padded over to the bathroom. Sure, Thaddeus was hot, with his messy hair, stubble, and dark brown eyes, but to have had such a vivid dream...what did that mean? As she turned on the taps and watched the hot water slosh into the bath, Winnie feared that just like she had tried to push him away in her dream, where she had secretly wanted him, she didn't want those feelings to become a reality.

"I can't allow that to happen," she whispered to herself. "I won't let it happen."

She hadn't come to Cornwall to settle down, to fall in love and live happily ever after. She didn't believe in fairy tales. Winnie only wanted to stay long enough to earn the money to pay rent on a place of her own. She wanted her own life – not somebody else's.

Winnie turned off the taps, stripped, and climbed into the bath. As she sunk beneath the water, she warned herself not to become too comfortable at the mansion, form any attachments, or grow roots. Roots kept you in one place. They stopped you from running away if you wanted or *needed* to. She closed her eyes and let the water wash over her.

Chapter Thirteen

Winnie stood in fresh panties and a bra, and worked her way through the clothes in the closets. All of the clothes were beautifully made. She went through each dress, skirt, top, trousers, and jeans, admiring their expensive quality. Although most of the clothes varied in style and fashion, most of them were coloured black, scarlet, violet, cream, or pale green. She paused over a couple of the garments and held them up to herself; they seemed to fit perfectly. Winnie pulled open the drawers in the base of the closet and found neat rows of shoes, trainers, and boots. She let her fingers dance over their suede and leather forms and as she did, Winnie noticed something which struck her as being very strange.

None of the shoes had ever been worn. She turned a couple of pairs over in her hands and studied each sole. They were in perfect condition. There wasn't one with a worn-down heel or scuffed toe in the whole collection. Winnie stood for a moment, hands on hips, and then turned back to the clothes. She pulled out different garments at random and searched their linings. To her amazement, all the clothing had the price tags still firmly fixed in place. Winnie found it a little curious but was also slightly relieved that none of the clothes had been worn. She hadn't relished the idea of wearing the clothes of a dead woman.

Shrugging to herself, she removed a sweater and a pair of jeans and pulled off the price tags. Dressed, she picked out a pair of trainers and slipped them on her feet. They fitted perfectly. Winnie closed the closet door and made her way downstairs. The kitchen clock read a quarter past nine as she filled the kettle and set about making herself some breakfast. The kettle bubbled away in the corner as she crossed to the window and peered out at the day before her. It was overcast again, but dry. She looked out across the patchwork of fields that spread away from the rear of the house and down to the sea. The house was so quiet, that if she listened really carefully, the faint sound of the waves crashing against the cliffs could be heard. Winnie had never known such silence before, and she thought back to the sounds she had heard in the wind as she had stood in the moonlight.

The kettle *clicked* off behind her, breaking the silence. She jumped at the sudden sound. Not wanting to dwell on what she thought she had seen and heard in the moonlight for fear of freaking herself out again, Winnie spied an iPod on the side and switched it on. Thumbing through the tracks, she noted that Thaddeus liked to listen to anything from Debussy to Maroon Five. Eventually, Winnie selected from the tracks, *Dance Again* by Jennifer Lopez. She kept the music low for fear of disturbing Thaddeus.

Swishing her butt from side to side to the music, Winnie fixed herself a steaming mug of coffee and a couple of slices of heavily buttered toast. When given the chance, she only ever toasted her bread on one side beneath a grill, because she loved the way the butter melted on its warm, golden surface and dripped through, making the bread all soft and doughy.

She finished her breakfast, placed her plate and mug in the sink, plucked the iPod from its dock, and put on the hooded coat Thaddeus had told her to wear the night before. With the money that Thaddeus had left on the table for her, she went into the hall. Just as she reached up on tiptoe to release the bolt that fastened the wide front doors shut, she noticed that the door to the lounge was open. Stepping away from the front door, Winnie peered into the lounge. Perhaps Thaddeus had risen early or had yet to go to bed.

"Thaddeus?" she called out.

Silence.

Then, as she stood in the open doorway, Winnie noticed that one of the comfy-looking armchairs had been moved, so it sat side on before one of the giant bay windows. Hanging over the back of the chair was a pretty violet top and a long, black skirt. Winnie stepped into the room and approached the chair. As she drew nearer, she could see that a book had been left perched on the arm of the chair. Picking it up, she turned it over in her hands and read the title.

"*The Lion, The Witch & The Wardrobe,*" she read aloud.

Then, as she was about to place the book back on the arm of the chair, a folded piece of paper slipped from between the pages of the book and fluttered to the floor. Winnie picked it up, unfolded it, and read what was scrawled across it.

Winnie,

I hope you don't think my choice of book is a little too young for you. I know you said that you aren't the best reader in the world, and I appreciate that you are eighteen years old, but this book is enjoyed by young and old alike. It truly is a magical story.

If you could kindly read from the book at dusk, while sitting in this chair by the window and wearing the clothes that I have left out for you, I would be very grateful.

I know that this may seem like a rather odd request, but I did warn you I had some little eccentricities.

Thank You,

Thad

Winnie read the note twice over, just in case her reading abilities were worse than she first thought and had misread the note left by Thaddeus.

After the second read, she folded the piece of paper in half again, and slid it back between the pages of the book.

"He's got to be kidding me," she sighed aloud. "What a freaking weirdo!"

She picked up the violet top and held it against her. Just like all the other clothing she had found, it looked like it would fit perfectly. Sighing, and not knowing what reason Thaddeus could have for wanting her to wear the clothes while sitting and reading the book, she laid the top over the back of the chair and left the room. She released the bolt and swung open the heavy front door. A pile of newspapers, as Thaddeus had mentioned, sat on the front step. They had been bound together with a length of white string. She hoisted them up, leaning to one side due to their sheer weight, and placed them in the hall as Thaddeus had requested. She swung the door shut behind her and made her way down into town.

Chapter Fourteen

Although the sun hung high in the sky like a copper disc, the air was fresh and it pinched her face. Winnie thrust her hands into her coat pockets, and plumes of wispy breath escaped through her mouth. She teetered every now and then on the rough ground, and she wished silently to herself for a little bit of tarmac. She wasn't used to the country life – not yet. Grey stone walls constructed crudely out of old rock and slate stood on either side of her. The land was broken up by these walls, and cut the fields up into uneven squares. The fields were a patchwork of different colours. Some green with rich, unkempt grass, others yellow-filled with wild gorse and several, a deep mauve with flowering heather. Winnie consumed all its rugged beauty and felt truly free at last.

Part of Winnie was glad that she had come to Cornwall with Thaddeus, but there was another part of her that told her she had made a mistake. It was like a little voice inside of her that just wouldn't stop whispering. The note which Thaddeus had left for her inside the book hadn't done anything to gag that voice. Why did he want her to sit in that particular chair, wearing those clothes, and reading that book? But the little voice was telling her it had something to do with Frances - Thaddeus's dead wife. Winnie knew that Thaddeus didn't want to speak about Frances, for every time she had raised the subject, he carefully steered her in another direction. She remembered Thaddeus telling her that she looked like his wife in some way.

That's it! Winnie thought to herself, as if tiny pieces of a puzzle had been slotted into place. Gooseflesh prickled her back. The clothes! His dead wife's clothes! Her coat, shoes, everything. He had coaxed her up to his house because she resembled Frances in some way, and by making her wear her clothes, Thaddeus was pretending that she was still alive – still with him.

That was kind of sick, right? Winnie thought. If not sick - creepy. She knew then why Thaddeus had left instructions for her to sit in that chair, wearing those clothes, and reading that book, because that's where Frances probably would have sat and read. He wanted to relive that moment of coming down the stairs and seeing his beloved Frances sitting quietly in the lounge, reading. But Winnie didn't want to be Frances and the whole idea of playing the role of a dead woman so Thaddeus didn't have to let go of his past, made her feel angry. She felt tricked by him. Housekeeper, my arse! She thought. The whole cooking thing, cleaning, washing and ironing his clothes - he didn't want a housekeeper – Thaddeus wanted a wife! He wanted Frances back. What would he expect her to do next for him? Sleep with him? And the thought made Winnie feel scared. Not of him, but what he might be expecting from her next.

Winnie didn't feel that Thaddeus was a bad man – she had been around plenty of those in the past to know what they were all about. She was beginning to wonder if Thaddeus wasn't a little crazy. Not dangerous crazy, but messed-up crazy, over the death of his wife. Shouldn't Thaddeus be coming to terms in some small way with his loss? After all, Thaddeus had told Winnie she had died about a year ago. Winnie understood loss, and she thought of her friend, Ruby Little. She had dealt with her death by trying not to think about Ruby; she had run away from that. Thaddeus hadn't, he seemed to be trapped, whereas Winnie had escaped. Either way, she guessed that neither Thaddeus nor she had dealt with their loss. So she couldn't really blame him for what he was trying to do. Winnie decided that she would do as he had requested, just this once, and take the opportunity to talk to him about Frances.

She made her way slowly through the town, pausing to look through the windows of the tiny shops which laid huddled together down the narrow streets. She discovered poky jewellery shops where earrings and necklaces had been fashioned out of shells washed up by the sea. Winnie passed tea shops and a little bakery where the intoxicating smell of fresh bread wafted on the cold sea air. A few knickknack shops were open, selling postcards and sweet rock. There was also the tiniest music shop she had ever seen, and she browsed around the small CD collection. Leaving the music shop, Winnie walked down onto the harbour where she discovered arcades which had been boarded up until the summer. She passed fish and chip shops and restaurants. She came across a row of shop fronts that had been turned into galleries, and she wandered amongst them, watching the artists at work as they lovingly painted pictures of the sea, boats, and fishermen hauling in their nets. One of the artists asked if Winnie wanted her portrait done in pastels while she waited. With a red flush on her cheeks, she declined and left the artist to his work. Seagulls swooped around her, calling out as they made their way out to sea. Fishermen worked on their boats down on the harbour, fixing, rigging, or preparing to set sail. She passed shops that sold fishing equipment, and she stopped for a while and watched live bait squirm and wriggle about in glass containers. After a time, Winnie came across the restaurant where she and Thaddeus had eaten the night before. Next to it was a small bookshop. Thinking of Thaddeus, Winnie pushed open the door and stepped inside.

A bell jingled above her head, and an old woman with a curved spine appeared from the back of the shop and shuffled to the front counter. Winnie noticed that her white hair was thinning and her pink scalp shone through in places. Nets of wrinkles had etched themselves around her crisp blue eyes and her puckered mouth. The old woman held a shawl tightly about her frame, and Winnie noticed that her hands were liver-spotted, and her fingers were gnarled and pinched together like chicken's feet. Gold-rimmed glasses hung about the woman's sagging neck on a chain. As she reached the counter, the old woman smiled sweetly at Winnie and said, "Good morning, my dear, how can I help you?"

Winnie returned the old lady's smile. "I just wondered if you sold any books of poetry."

The old woman nodded. "Yes, my dear, I do have a small selection. Mostly classics, really." She stepped from behind the counter and began to make her way through the shop. "Come this way and I'll show you what I have."

"Thank you," Winnie smiled, and followed the old lady to the rear of the shop. They stopped before a row of shelves which adorned the wall before them. The old woman popped her spectacles onto the bridge of her nose and peered at the spines of the books. She ran a shaking hand along the row.

"Were you looking for any poet in particular, or perhaps a collection of love sonnets for such a beautiful young lady as yourself?"

Winnie blushed and said, "I'm looking for some poetry by a poet named Thaddeus Blake."

The old woman looked thoughtfully for a moment and then began to shake her head. "There's William Blake, but I can't say I've ever heard of a poet called Thaddeus Blake, my sweet. You did say Thaddeus Blake, didn't you?"

"Yes," Winnie nodded.

The old woman continued to shake her head thoughtfully, "Now that's a new name to me. Does he write modern verse?"

Winnie began to get a little confused now. She knew she didn't know enough about poetry to discuss the differing styles that seemed to exist. To her, a poem was a bunch of words that rhymed.

"I'm not sure," Winnie said.

The old woman smiled again, "Not to worry, my dear. I'll check on the Internet for you." She turned and made her way back to the front counter.

"There really isn't any need to go to any trouble," Winnie called after her.

"Hush, hush now, my dear. It really isn't any trouble," the old woman smiled, reaching the counter where there was a computer.

While Winnie waited for the old woman to check her database, she looked at all the rows of books. She wondered about all the words printed in the shop and the stories they told. As she stood and thought about all the different stories created by all the different writers in the world, she knew she would love to have a look at one of Thaddeus's books of poetry. She would find it a curious thing to hold it in her hands and look over all the neatly printed words. She thought it must be a very precious thing indeed to have written a book, to which people you had never met, would read and share your words and ideas. Winnie wanted a copy of Thaddeus's poems so she could see what words and ideas he had wanted to share with others.

The old woman looked up from the computer and said, "I'm sorry, dear, but there doesn't seem to be a record of any such poet. You did say Thaddeus Blake, didn't you?"

Winnie just nodded, disappointed and confused.

"Well he just doesn't exist. There isn't any such poet, my dear," the old woman smiled.

She thanked the woman for her help, and with a frown, Winnie left the bookshop.

Chapter Fifteen

Winnie spent the next hour or so buying the groceries which Thaddeus had asked for. She went about this chore systematically as her mind puzzled over what the old woman in the bookshop had told her.

Again, Winnie had become suspicious of Thaddeus, but she wondered if there wasn't an explanation, how crazy or weird, why he didn't come up on the shopkeeper's database. Okay, so Thaddeus had told her he was a poet and that's what he spent his nights alone writing. As he had explained himself the very first night that they had met, he liked the peace and quiet of the night and the solitude it provided. So maybe his writing was no more than a hobby? Then again, hadn't he said his reason for being in London was to meet with his publisher? She wondered. Perhaps he wasn't yet published? But this just only filled Winnie's head with more questions about her eccentric employer. Like she planned to ask him about Frances, she decided to also tell Thaddeus about her uneventful visit to the bookshop. Winnie paid for the groceries in the supermarket, and left. Her mind was so muddled with her own thoughts, that she missed the newspaper stand outside with its bold black headline, which read: *Local woman and baby found butchered.*

As Winnie made her way back up the hill with the heavy bags of groceries swinging from her fists, she knew she would have to be careful how she raised the issues of his dead wife and the bookshop visit. Thaddeus was her employer after all, and he might not be too happy if he thought she had been snooping on him. Although Winnie's suspicions had been raised, she still needed the job until she had raised enough money to run again.

As she stood and unpacked the shopping in the kitchen and stored it away in the cupboards, Winnie pushed her doubts and fears to the back of her mind. She would deal with them later - when Thaddeus woke. Winnie fixed herself a ham sandwich for lunch and relaxed at the kitchen table with a cup of coffee and a packet of Cadbury's chocolate fingers she had added to the groceries.

An hour later she set about cleaning the house. Winnie found a duster and a can of polish in a cupboard beneath the kitchen sink and moved through the dining room. She dusted and polished the long table until its surface was gleaming. Wiping away the dust which had built up around the window frames, she decided that if the weather was warmer tomorrow, she would venture outside and clean the windows. The window by the chair she was going to sit and read in was particularly grubby she noticed, and you could barely see out of it. Winnie walked around the room, dusting the bookshelves and knocking away the beginnings of cobwebs that had crept between the books. She figured that dust and cobwebs must be a continuing problem in a house this size, and once she had finished cleaning all of the rooms, she would have to start right back at the beginning again.

Winnie spent an hour or more just dusting the dining room and by the time she had finished, her arms and back ached. The pain clawed its way across her shoulder blades and dug at the small of her back. She hung her arms loosely by her sides, rolling her shoulders and stretching her spine as she left the dining room and crossed the hall. Winnie reached the door which led into the lounge and paused. She backtracked a few paces and stood before the oil painting in the hall which hung opposite the picture of Thaddeus. She stared up at the picture, letting her eyes travel over the painted face before her. The woman's face was a little longer and narrower than her own, but the colour of her hair and eyes matched Winnie's. The women in the painting did look a lot like her. With her flesh breaking out in goose bumps, Winnie knew that she was looking at a painting of Frances. Then, as she slowly passed the paintings of the other women, she thought with a strange disquiet, that in an uncanny way, she looked a little like all of them. Not knowing if her imagination was working overtime and that she was now becoming suspicious of everything and anything connected to Thaddeus, Winnie told herself not to be so dumb and turned her back on the paintings of Frances and the other women. To try and clear her mind of her nagging doubts and ever-growing paranoia, Winnie took the iPod, put in the earphones, and spent the rest of the afternoon cleaning the lounge and kitchen while listening to *Alone Again* By Alyssa Reid as loud as she could bear.

At about five p.m., Winnie noticed that the house had begun to grow dim as the winter sunlight began to fade over the hill. She passed through the house, switching on lights. In the lounge, she switched on the lamp next to the chair where she had been asked to sit and read. Taking the clothes from the back of the chair, she made her way upstairs to get changed into them. In her room, Winnie discarded the clothes she had been wearing that day, placing them in the laundry basket along with the rest of her dirty clothes. It was then Winnie noticed the blouse with Thaddeus's bloody handprint on it and she wondered if the cut had now healed.

Winnie put on the violet top and black skirt Thaddeus had left out for her. She found a black pair of shoes with a small heel amongst the many other pairs in the closet. Setting her hair and her makeup, she stood before the mirror and wondered if this was really how Frances had looked when she was living and breathing. Desperate not to spook herself out, Winnie left her room and made her way down the landing.

As she moved along the wide corridor with its many doors, she noticed that one of them was slightly ajar. She stopped outside. No light came from within. Winnie tapped lightly on the door with her knuckles. There was no response from inside. Glancing quickly back over her shoulder, she gently pushed open the door and ventured inside.

Chapter Sixteen

The room was in complete darkness. Winnie fumbled with her hand along the wall and flipped on the light switch. A single bulb overhead cast a glow of pale light into the room. Winnie went to the windows to draw back the thick, heavy curtains which hung over them. She pulled them back and a shower of dust fell from them. The curtains smelt musty and old, as if they hadn't been aired for some time. Then, much to her dismay, Winnie discovered that the windows behind the curtain had been boarded over with planks of wood. Each piece has been fastened to the window frame with several nails. With a frown across her brow, she turned and looked at the room. It was poky. Probably one of the smallest rooms in the house, she thought. The air in the room smelt stale and rancid, and she screwed up her nose. A narrow bed lay against the far wall. Beside it there was an ancient-looking rocking chair. A small wooden table sat opposite the chair with an old-fashioned Singer sewing machine. Winnie went over to the table. Looking closely at the sewing machine, she discovered it worked manually by turning a small wheel which protruded from one end, and with the aid of a wooden pedal that lay on the floor beneath the table. A velvet-covered needlework box lay beside the ancient machine and very delicately, Winnie lifted its lid. Reels of fine cotton and lace lay neatly in the box and she ran her fingers gingerly over them. Needles, threads, old buttons, and china thimbles were also neatly placed inside. Winnie lowered the lid and turned around. Across from her was a dressing table, which looked like some kind of antique. There was a hairbrush with coarse yellow bristles and a marble back which had been decorated with gold, along with a powder puff and silver hairgrips. A china statue of a ballerina stood gracefully to one side. Winnie picked it up and felt its cool surface. She held it close in the dim lighting so she could marvel at its fine beauty. Holding it close to her face, she could see it was covered with tiny blue cracks. After a few moments of study, she placed it back in its original position. A row of drawers were carved into the dressing table, and curling her fingers around one of the gold handles, she eased one of them open. Winnie reached inside and pulled out some photographs.

Holding them up in the light, Winnie studied the pictures. The first was a recent colour photograph of a frail old woman. By the look of her sallow, paper-thin skin, Winnie guessed her age to be at least ninety, maybe even older than that. Her hair was white and wispy, and it stood out from her narrow skull like springs. Dark smudges of age and ill health coloured the weighty bags of flesh which hung beneath her watery eyes. Deep lines of age ravaged her face, giving her a drawn and pointed look. Studying the picture, Winnie wondered if it wasn't a picture of Thaddeus's grandmother. There was another picture, again of the old woman, taken in the room which Winnie now found herself in. The old woman was stooped forward in the rocking chair and she was staring up out of the photo. Winnie turned to the next photograph. Again, this was of the old woman. She was seated in a wheelchair, outside the house. It was dark and if it hadn't have been for the shaft of moonlight, Thaddeus, who stood beside the woman in this picture, would have been hidden in shadow. His right hand was rested on her left shoulder. A smile danced across both of their lips.

"What are you doing in here?" Thaddeus suddenly asked from behind her.

Winnie jumped, sending the photographs spilling to the floor. She spun around to face him as he stood in the doorway. "Hey, Thaddeus, you made me jump," she breathed.

Thaddeus crossed the room, his dark eyes fixed firmly upon hers. As he drew near, Winnie saw that tonight the colour of his eyes were almost black. He stopped before her, and stooping, he bent down and gathered up the photographs. Thaddeus placed them back in the drawer and shut it.

"What are you doing in here?" he asked again, his eyes never leaving hers.

"I saw that the door was ajar and thought maybe you were in here," she mumbled, feeling like a thief who had been caught stealing.

"Well as you can now see, I wasn't," he said, searching her eyes. Winnie looked past him and gesturing towards the dressing table drawer, she said, "Those photographs, Thaddeus, were they of your grandmother?"

"Yes," he replied, his voice flat.

"Where is she now?" Winnie pushed.

"Look, Winnie, I am not discussing this any further with you," he said, his voice not angry but firm. "I've warned you I have my eccentric ways and requests, and one of them is that you're never to enter this room again. It is private. You have no business in here."

Winnie tried to ease her way out of the uncomfortable situation she was now faced with and said, "Thaddeus, I wasn't snooping around. Like I said, the door was open, and I didn't know I wasn't meant to come in here. I'm sorry."

Thaddeus's eyes began to defreeze and warm slowly. "Well now you do know, so please don't come in here again."

Winnie gave him a half-smile and Thaddeus gestured her back towards the open door. On the landing again, Thaddeus closed the door behind them. Then looking her up and down, he said, "Thank you for wearing the clothes I left out for you."

Feeling self-conscious as Thaddeus eyed her, Winnie ran the flat of her hands down the side of the skirt, straightening any creases that might be there. "I hope I look okay?"

"You look more than okay," he said thoughtfully, his eyes never leaving her. "You look perfect. Now, if you wouldn't mind, I'd be grateful if you would go and sit by the window and read just like I asked you to."

Chapter Seventeen

Thaddeus followed Winnie into the lounge where she took her seat in the chair positioned by the window, and picked up the book. It was now pitch dark outside and Winnie caught a glimpse of her reflection in the grimy window. The wind howled outside and the panes of glass rattled in their frames. She looked down at the first page of the book and the rows and rows of words. So many at once seemed rather daunting to her, and she felt uncomfortable dressed like she was. It was hard to concentrate. She read the first few lines slowly, and then sneaked a glance up at Thaddeus. He had taken one of the newspapers which had been delivered, and was now sitting on the sofa opposite her and reading.

Over the top of the book, she spied on him as he sat cross-legged, in faded blue denims and a shirt. His hair stood up as if he had been caught in a storm, but as ever, his dark eyes were bright and keen as he read the paper. Although he looked no older than twenty-five years old, Thaddeus had an air about him - an arrogance, Winnie thought - that made him appear older. For someone so young, he brimmed with confidence.

"Are you enjoying the book?" he suddenly asked without looking up.

"Erm, yeah, it's great," she said, looking back down at the book.

"I'd be surprised if you had even read one page," he smiled behind his newspaper so she couldn't see.

"And what makes you think that?" she asked, peering once again over the top of the book at him.

"Because you've been too preoccupied with looking at me," he said from behind his newspaper.

Closing the book, Winnie scowled and said, "Why do you have to be so...so..." she trailed off, unable to think of the word she wanted.

"Good looking?" And now his smile turned to a grin, hidden by the paper.

"*Weird*, was the word I was actually thinking of," she said slamming the book shut.

"Weird?" he said, now peering at her over the top of his newspaper. "What's that supposed to mean?"

"Nothing," she said, opening the book again and staring down at the words.

"You can't just make a statement like that and not explain yourself," he said, closing his newspaper and placing it to one side.

Winnie sensed that he was more curious than pissed off, so placing the book in her lap, she looked straight at him and said, "Thaddeus, why have you got me dressed in these clothes and reading this book?"

"Why not?" he shrugged.

Winnie thought she noticed just a glimmer of his self-belief and confidence melt away at her question. "Because it's *weird*, that's why," she gasped.

"Why is it so weird?" he frowned. "You are very pretty. Am I not allowed to ask you to wear pretty clothes, so that I may admire you? You bring a certain radiance to this sometimes glum and gloomy place."

"But you're not admiring me," she said sounding exasperated. "You're reading the freaking newspaper!"

"So you want me to sit and stare at you?" he said, folding his arms and looking straight at her, a broad grin on his face.

"Please just tell me the real reason," she breathed. "If I am to stay and carry on working for you, then I need to understand some of these *strange* ways that you have, or I'm just gonna get freaked out and run again."

"Would you really run?" he asked her, his smile faltering just a fraction. "Where would you run to? Back to London? Would you really walk out on a job, money, a place to live..."

"If I was scared enough," she whispered.

"Do I scare you?" he asked, the smile almost gone now.

"No," she said thoughtfully. "But this dressing up thing is, like, really weird and I'm not sure that I'm comfortable with it."

"What could be uncomfortable about wearing expensive clothes..." he started.

"Because they're your dead wife's clothes," Winnie blurted out. Part of her immediately wanted to clap her hand over her mouth and swallow those words, but that little part of her - the one that whispered sometimes - was glad she had said what she had.

"Then we'll buy replacements," Thaddeus said.

"And I bet they'll be exact copies of what I'm wearing now," she said.

"What of it?" he shrugged.

Then taking a deep breath and swallowing hard, Winnie said, "Thaddeus, I'm not Frances. I'm not your dead wife. My name is Winter McCall, I was born in the back of an ambulance during the middle of a snowstorm, I ran away from home and became homeless. I didn't move here with you so I could pretend to be someone else."

"With a backstory like that, I thought you'd be grateful of the chance to be someone else," he shot back.

Hardly able to believe what he had just said, Winnie's mouth dropped open. "You fucking nob!" she hissed, throwing the book on the floor and jumping up. "I've had enough of this bullshit!"

Winnie ran from the room and went to the front door. She reached for the handle, but before she had the chance to pull the door open, Thaddeus slammed his hand against it.

"Don't go," he said.

And just like she had seen the night before, Winnie saw that desperation in his eyes again.

"What, stay here and let you take the piss out of me?" she sneered. This time she was too angry to cry. "No thanks!"

"I'm sorry," he whispered.

"Yeah, I've heard that my whole life," she snapped back. "It means shit!"

"Please just let me explain," Thaddeus implored her. He reached for her hands, and she jerked them away.

"Don't touch me!" she barked.

Then raising his hands in the air as if in surrender, he said, "Okay, but please just let me explain before you go. I think I owe you that at least."

"Explain what, exactly?" she glared at him.

"Why I really invited you to come and stay with me," he said.

Chapter Eighteen

Winnie followed Thaddeus back into the lounge. He gestured for her to sit back in the chair by the window again. Winnie sat on the edge of the seat, not eagerly awaiting him to tell his story, but just in case she needed to jump up and leave quickly. Thaddeus sat opposite her on the sofa, pulling up his legs and crossing them. He sat forward, his wrists hanging over his knees, his head slightly forward. The wind howled outside and the windows rattled in their frames again. Thaddeus looked up as if glancing out of the window, then looked at Winnie.

"I'm sorry," he stated. "You were right about me and I'm so very sorry. If you feel that you still want to leave after I have explained why I brought you here, you will receive no quarrel from me and you can leave when you wish."

"What are you sorry for?" Winnie asked, her temper fading slightly.

Thaddeus stared at her through the glow of the lamp and said, "I watched you for seven nights. I saw you by chance one evening. After having dinner with my publisher, we went our separate ways. I had one night left in London and it wasn't a particularly cold evening, so I decided to take a walk along the Embankment and watch the boats pass along the river. I sat for a while to smoke a cigarette or two, and it was then I saw you. You were sitting on the steps outside the Embankment Tube Station, and my heart almost stopped at once as I peered through the passing traffic at you. At first I thought I was seeing a ghost. I thought you were Frances."

To hear him say this, Winnie shuddered inside and felt cold all over.

Thaddeus took a cigarette from the silver case in his pocket and lit one. Smoke curled up from the corner of his mouth, and he watched Winnie through the coils of blue smoke.

"I couldn't move from that seat, Winnie," he started to explain again. "It was like I was frozen in time somehow. This time last year, I had watched Frances be eaten away by cancer, only to see her again before my very eyes, sitting across the road from me. Was it some cruel trick, or my imagination? But as I sat and watched you, I realised that you were, in fact, not her. Your resemblance is uncanny – but there are subtle differences. With my heart heavy in my chest, and old feelings reawakened within me, I hurried back to my hotel. It was like my brain had a fever. I was almost delirious with madness. My brain had become haunted by memories of Frances. When I closed my eyes, all I could see was you, Winnie, sitting in the dark and cold, holding your hands out, begging strangers for money.

"You seemed to be so alike in looks that I even began to wonder if Frances had had some secret sister, a relative that she had failed to tell me about. In my heart, I knew that not to be true. I telephoned the hotel lobby and told them that I would be staying several more nights," he said, drawing deeply on his cigarette.

"Why?" Winnie asked him.

"I didn't know at the time," he said, glancing back at the window as rain now beat against it. "I spent the day beneath the covers of the hotel bed, fearing to shut my eyes in case you were there again. Then, whether through tiredness or madness, I decided to take another walk along the Embankment again that night. I didn't know why, I had no plan, other than I needed to see you again. I had to make sure that you weren't really Frances, however insane that seemed. After a very light evening meal, as I felt too sick to eat, I made my way back to the Embankment. I sat on the bench on the opposite side of the road and watched the entrance of the station. After the time it took for me to smoke almost half a pack of cigarettes, you appeared. Again, I spied on you as you begged those people in their expensive suits for money. It almost broke my heart to see you doing that."

"Why?" Winnie cut in. "You didn't know me. I meant nothing to you."

"It was Frances I could see begging," he said, crushing out his cigarette and lighting another. "It wasn't you I could see in that scruffy sweater, filthy jeans, and trainers. It was like I was watching my Frances shuffling back and forth, starving, cold, and hungry. It almost tore my heart in two to watch you night after night."

"So you came back every night?" Winnie asked, not feeling creeped out, but kind of sad for him. She pitied him.

"Every night," he said, and then looked away as if in shame. "But what was I to do? I knew in my heart that you weren't Frances – I had accepted that by night three, I think. I didn't want to leave you there. It was like I owed it to Frances in some way not to leave you behind. To return to my home and its fineries would have driven me half mad. How could I have rested or settled knowing that someone, who so reminded me of the person I loved more than anything, was living such a pitiful existence? Was I to snatch you off the street? I was not prepared to commit a crime. Approach you, explain everything, and then ask you to come and live with me? You would have thought me mad. As I watched you rebuke those men who approached you, I knew how I could get you to leave London."

"How?" Winnie asked him, sensing that she had now been manipulated in some way and feeling uncomfortable about it.

"I could see that you had your dignity – your pride," he explained. "People like that don't accept charity, and it was then the idea struck me. I would offer you a job. A job brings pride, a sense of worth – it has honesty about it. It was a deal that we could both benefit from."

Staring at him wide-eyed, Winnie said, "The job, the wage, and a roof over my head is how I would benefit, but how would you?" she asked, suspecting she already knew the answer.

"I got to be reminded everyday of Frances," he said, looking away again in shame as his true motives were revealed. Then, with his head still turned from her, he added, "I wouldn't blame you for thinking me mad, even sinister perhaps, but there you have it – you have the truth."

Winnie drew a deep breath, and although her suspicions had been proved right, it did nothing to silence the growing disquiet she felt inside her. "I don't think you are mad or sinister," she finally said. "But you are grieving, and perhaps you should go and talk to someone about it. What you've done, and what you are doing, by asking me to dress like your dead wife so you can remember her, isn't exactly normal."

"I've read many stories where those who have lost loved ones have never been able to throw away their clothes, possessions," he said, as if trying to justify his actions. "Some people have even left their loved ones' rooms exactly as they were on the day they died."

"And those people, I guess, lead incredibly sad lives," she said, the anger and frustration in her voice now gone. She found it hard to muster any anger towards Thaddeus as he sat opposite her with sadness in his eyes that she knew she had seen before. Ruby Little had often had such a haunted look when she returned from the alleyways – from being with those men. It was like a piece of her soul was missing. Just as those men had taken a little piece of Ruby's soul, Frances had taken a piece of Thaddeus's the day she died. "The people you describe, Thaddeus, never move on with their lives."

"Run away, you mean?" he said looking up at her. "Because that's what you do, Winnie. You don't confront your problems, either."

"Perhaps not," she said thoughtfully.

"We are more alike than you think," he said, putting out the cigarette which had now burnt down to the butt. "Maybe in a way I didn't first consider, we could help each other."

"I don't think by parading around the house in your dead wife's clothes are going to help either of us very much," she said back.

"I'll buy you some new clothes," he said.

"But that's the point," she sighed. "I don't want you to buy me new clothes. I want to be able to buy my own. Be my own person for once in my life, and not what everyone else expects me to be."

"And you will be able to buy your own clothes with the wage I pay you," he said. "It's not charity, Winnie, it's a job. You will work for your money. You will earn every penny."

Winnie thought of the eight hundred pounds he had offered to pay her each month, and with no rent to pay, nor bills, she knew that it wouldn't take her very long to be able to save enough money to be able to pay the deposit and the first month's rent on a place of her own. Then she really would be free and would never have to run again. With her own address, she would be able to get a proper job and finally live like everyone else did.

"What do you say?" he half-smiled at her, but again she could see that desperation in his eyes. "I promise. No more dressing up, no more pretending you are Frances."

"But why do you want me to stay, if the reason you brought me here was that I reminded you of..." Winnie stared.

"You will still remind me of her," he confessed. "There is no denying that. Over the last few days since you came to stay here, I have realised grief isn't the only thing eating a hole in me."

"What do you mean?" Winnie asked.

"Loneliness," he said. "I have enjoyed your company very much. You might look like Frances, but your personalities are very different. You have a feistiness about you, and although you have lead a difficult life, you have retained a naivety which I like very much. You are great company and I would hate to go back to wandering this vast house on my own. I have found a great comfort in knowing that you are around."

Winnie listened to his gentle voice, and again she found herself being captivated by it, just like she had the night he had approached her on the Embankment. Then, thinking back to their first meeting, she thought of the life she had once led. It already seemed like a lifetime ago, and she didn't want to go back to that any more than Thaddeus wanted to go back to being lonely.

Thaddeus watched her thoughtfully.

"Will you stay then?" he asked her. "Give me another chance now that I have been honest with you."

Winnie drew a deep breath and said, "Okay, I will stay – for now. Although, I won't be Frances's ghost."

"Understood," he half-smiled at her. "We have a deal then?"

"I guess," she whispered.

"Excellent," he smiled. Then standing up, he looked at her and added, "If I remember rightly, I thought I said I was going to cook tonight."

"You said you were going to teach me how to cook," she reminded him as she stood up. "You didn't like the fish fingers, remember?"

"Let's get started then," he smiled at her.

Then, before leaving the lounge, he went to the window where Winnie had been sitting. He closed the curtains and switched out the lamp, throwing the room into darkness.

Chapter Nineteen

In the kitchen, Winnie filled the kettle with water and switched it on, then started to prepare two mugs of coffee.

"I think tonight calls for something a little stronger than coffee," Thaddeus said, switching off the kettle. He went to the fridge and took out a bottle of white wine. There was silence between them as he poured them both a glass. He handed one to her, and smiling he said, "A new beginning for both of us."

Winnie smiled then took a sip from her glass. She watched Thaddeus go back to the fridge and sort through the groceries she had bought earlier that day. As the light from the fridge fell upon his face, Winnie couldn't help but think, that, while he looked no older than twenty-five, he had a way about him – a maturity – which gave her the impression he was older. She continued to sip her wine and watch him as he took out some chicken breasts and a tub of plain yogurt and placed them on the table. Her eyes never left him as he crossed to one of the cupboards above the worktop and retrieved a cooking apple, an onion, and a clove of garlic, then placed them alongside the chicken and yogurt. He then turned to the spice rack and plucked four little bottles from it. He placed these on the table along with a cube of chicken stock and a bottle of cooking oil.

As Winnie stood and slowly drank the wine, she wondered how Thaddeus knew how to cook so well. She guessed that most guys his age would struggle to cook a pizza without burning it, yet here he was, busying himself in the kitchen and putting together all the ingredients for what she knew would be something far grander than the fish fingers she had served up.

With a smile tugging at the corner of his full lips, and with what looked like a flicker of excitement in his eyes, he said, "Winnie, tonight I'm going to teach you to cook one of my favourite dishes, Bramley Turkey Korma."

"I didn't buy any turkey," she said.

"Not to worry," he assured her. "Chicken is just as good."

He turned, drew a large slender knife from a rack on the work surface. He unwrapped the chicken breasts, and like a surgeon, he quickly sliced the meat into thin slivers. He spoke to her as he worked and said, "Get a pan from the cupboard over there and heat some oil"

Winnie did as he asked, placing a pan on the stove and pouring in some of the cooking oil. She found herself beginning to enjoy working alongside Thaddeus. She had never done anything like this with anyone before. He stood close to her, and placing the slivers of chicken into the hot pan, he said, "We have to sauté the chicken first."

"Sauté?" she frowned, enjoying being taught by him.

He smiled at her and she could tell he was enjoying himself, too, and she now hoped the misunderstandings between them could be put behind them.

"We need to seal all the juices and flavour of the chicken into the meat," he explained.

Thaddeus took a plate out of a cupboard and placed it on the work surface beside the oven. "Can you get me a fork out of the drawer, please, Winnie?"

She found one and handed it to him. Thaddeus plucked the meat from the pan with the fork and placed it on the plate. Winnie watched him carefully. He crossed back to the table, and tossing her the onion, he said, "Peel and slice that." Winnie set about the task, cutting the onion in half.

With a sideways glance, he looked at her, and with a smile, he said, "Are you crying?"

"It's this onion," she smiled and sniffed.

Then standing before her, Thaddeus wiped the tears from her face with his thumb. Winnie felt awkward and turned her face away. "It's okay, I can do it," she said.

"Sorry," Thaddeus smiled, looking embarrassed. "I could just see that you had your hands full so I thought I would..."

"No, it's okay, honest," Winnie blushed and went back to slicing the onion.

When Winnie was done, Thaddeus added the onion to the pan, leaving it to simmer. Winnie sat at the table and sipped her wine as Thaddeus began to boil some rice. As he worked, Winnie told him about her trip into town and her visit to the bookshop. With his back to her, Thaddeus listened to her story. After she had finished, he picked up his glass of wine, drank a mouthful and said, "You wouldn't find any poetry books by a poet named Thaddeus Blake. The old woman in the shop was right. He doesn't exist."

With a frown, Winnie said, "But you told me you were a poet and that's what you did as a job."

Thaddeus plucked the bottled spices from the table and tipped a little of each into the simmering pan. He then began to cut the clove of garlic into paper-thin slices.

"It's not how I make a living," he said. Then just as Winnie had suspected, he added, "The money that I have has all been inherited. It's more of a hobby, really, but I write under a pseudonym."

"A pseudonym?"

"Yes. It's a fancy word for a pen name."

"Why would you want to do that?" she asked him.

"For two reasons," he said, adding the garlic to the pan. "Firstly, there is a far better poet than myself named Blake, albeit his first name was William, and secondly, I'd like to keep my identity a secret. I don't write for the money, I have inherited enough. I don't write to collect adoring fans, and I definitely don't write for fame."

"Why do it then?" Winnie asked, and then drank the last of the wine in her glass.

Leaving the pan to simmer, Thaddeus refilled Winnie's glass and sat at the table.

"I write because I love words. The pictures, the images you can create with them. Poetry gives me a chance to play with words, sculpt them into something beautiful," he tried to explain to her.

"But I don't understand. If you have something to say, why not say it instead of using posh, fancy words?" she asked.

A touch of a smile played out across his lips. "Winnie, stand up," he said.

She continued to sit for a moment, a little unsure of herself as he watched her.

"Go on," he said.

Slowly she got up and stood before him. She felt uncomfortable, as if she was on show somehow.

"Now, Winnie, what are you wearing?" he asked her.

She frowned, and then said, "Clothes?"

He smiled as he sat back in his seat, his eyes never leaving hers. "What is their purpose?"

"To cover my body? To keep me warm?" she said, feeling kind of dumb.

"Exactly," Thaddeus beamed. "So if those clothes are made to cover your body and keep you warm, why do they have such beautiful colours, designs, and fastenings? Wouldn't they serve their purpose just as well without all of the added extras?"

"Yeah, but they look prettier like this. They'd be boring and dull otherwise," she said.

Thaddeus clapped his hands together. "And it would be the same with words, Winnie." Then standing up, and looking at her, he said, "Why just write, 'the woman was beautiful.' Why was she beautiful? Is it the colour of her hair, her eyes? Is it her complexion?" he asked, as if studying her. "I use words to create pictures in another's mind. I want words to work magic."

"I never thought about words like that before," she said, looking back at him.

Then turning his back on her, Thaddeus picked up the yogurt pot and poured its contents into the pan. He mixed it in with a wooden spoon. While stirring, he turned to face her as she sat back down at the table.

Winnie took another sip of the wine, then said, "Thaddeus, can you show me one of your books? I'd love to see one."

Thaddeus knew he had caught her imagination, and she was relaxing with the aid of the wine. He didn't want Winnie to put up her guard again. So smiling at her, he said, "If you serve up dinner, I'll go and see if I can't find a copy of one of my books."

Thaddeus left the kitchen, and Winnie placed the plates of steaming food on the table with a set of knives and forks for the both of them. She looked up to see Thaddeus standing in the doorway. In his hand he was holding a book. He passed it to her and sat down at the table.

Winnie turned the book over in her hands and read the front: *Frances by Jonathan Whitby.* She opened the book and thumbed delicately through the pages. She gazed over the neat rows of printed text. She looked across at Thaddeus, who was eating the food they had cooked together.

"Read me one of your poems," she said.

"Why?" he smiled, and now he looked a little embarrassed.

Winnie didn't feel comfortable telling him that he had a voice like silk, so she simply said, "Why not?"

Laying his knife and fork beside his plate, Thaddeus reached across and took the book of poems from her hands. He flicked through the pages with his long fingers, stopped, cleared his throat, and began to read to her.

The heart beats like Indian calls and castanets
Upon the first time our touch first met
Strange creatures danced with costumes fair
As we shook the dreams from our hair
Our laughter cast ripples into the dawn
As we smiled away our final yawn
Floating on a breeze of bliss
We stole just one last kiss

Come into these arms again
And cry a gentle sigh
Eyelashes of pure lace
Pulling cobwebs from the eye
Peeling off skins from the past
Glorifying a new self

Saddened creases about my smiles
Trying to hide myself

With the sound of Thaddeus's voice almost seeming to float about the room, and the wine she had drank, Winnie's head began to swim.
She sat captivated by him as he continued.

Angels know your secrets
In which you trust in me
You know from where I came
As they fly from you to me
Playing with impassioned words
On a bed of rust
Swathed in your dying blankets
I've found a love to trust
Listen to the words
I write, plant, and sew
With eyes of wonder we sit and watch
As they flower so
At night we cower beneath the ancient moon
And you fear what will happen
If they come to soon

Such peace I have found inside your love
This time seems too insane
But love is like sweet mistletoe
With its beauty and its pain

Thaddeus slowly closed the book and set it down beside him. Without looking at Winnie, he picked up his knife and fork and started to eat.

Winnie felt as if she had been put under a spell. After some time, she didn't how long, she said, "Thaddeus, that was the most beautiful poem. I'm not sure exactly what it all meant, but you were writing about how much you loved Frances."

He looked up from his meal and met her gaze. Although he was smiling, Winnie could see his eyes had grown dull and were full of sadness.

"You must have loved Frances so much," she whispered, and wondered if anyone would ever write a poem about her.

"Yes, I did. I was captivated by her from the very first moment I saw her. It was like I had loved her always, since time began."

"The oil painting hanging in the hall, the one facing you, is that Frances?" she asked.

"Yes," he said, just above a whisper.

"And the others?"

Thaddeus straightened in his seat a little, his eyes growing brighter now. "The paintings of the men are my forefathers, and the women are their wives."

"The women all look very much the same. Auburn hair, green eyes, and pale skin," she said.

A smile lingered across his lips, and he said, "All of the men in my family have been able to recognise a beautiful woman when they saw one. Besides, we are all related. It's common for men from the same bloodline to find similar looking women attractive."

They sat in silence. The only sound was the clacking of their knives and forks as they ate. Once she was full, Winnie pushed her plate to one side and picked up the glass of wine. She sipped from it, and then broke the silence. "You are the strangest man I have ever met."

"Should I take that as compliment?" he asked, pushing his own plate aside.

"Take it any way you like," she smiled.

"I'm not so strange," he said.

As Winnie sat and tried to understand the man sitting before her, she knew there was a little part of her which envied the love that Frances and Thaddeus must have shared. She had never known anything like that. However strange she thought of him, Winnie accepted his reasons. Perhaps if she had ever known love like he had, she might have had the same difficulty coming to terms with their death. He had explained about how he afforded to live, the paintings in the hallway, and the reason why the old woman in the bookshop had never heard of him. Winnie looked at him, and couldn't help but feel a little guilty at the distrust she had felt. She had never met anyone she could trust before. Even her friend, Ruby Little, used to steal from her. Was her lack of trust in people, Thaddeus's fault? No, she thought. It was hers.

Thaddeus caught her staring at him and said, "What?"

"You might be strange, Thaddeus, but you're a nice guy," she said. "Thank you, for dinner."

"I should be the one thanking you," he said back.

"What for?" she asked him.

"For agreeing to stay," he said, standing up. He took their empty plates and placed them in the sink.

Winnie turned to look at him, and she noticed that he seemed to be staring intently out of the window. She could see his reflection in the pane of glass. Winnie couldn't be sure if it was just the way his face was reflecting back in the window, which like the others she had noticed, were covered in dirt, but he looked scared. He looked as if he had seen a ghost.

"What are you looking at?" she asked, getting up from the table, curious to know what it was he was staring at through the dirty windowpane.

Before she had joined him, Thaddeus had drawn the curtains over the window. He turned to face her and said, "The rain looks like it is easing and the moon is up. I think I might go outside and get some air."

Leaving Winnie alone, Thaddeus left the kitchen.

Chapter Twenty

Winnie took the grey coat with the hood from the hook on the back of the kitchen door and left the room. She crossed the hallway to find the front door open. A chill breeze blew into the hall, bringing with it a flurry of sodden leaves. Winnie peered out into the darkness and could see that it was still raining slightly. Thaddeus was standing in front of the house, his hands by his sides. His head was tilted back and he was looking up into the half-moon that peered behind a wisp of grey cloud. The moonbeams splashed his face, as did the fine rain.

Pulling the coat tight about herself, Winnie stepped out of the house and stood next to Thaddeus. He looked at her, and seeing that she was getting wet, he gently pulled the hood up over her head. "You don't want to get a cold," he said over the sound of the wind that blew around the eaves of the house and between the branches of the trees. Winnie peered into the thick slices of black between their twisted trunks, and she remembered the three pale, white faces she feared she had seen before.

"Isn't it beautiful?" Thaddeus breathed.

"Say what?" Winnie asked, looking away from the tree line and sideways at Thaddeus.

"The moonlight," he said again, staring up into the thin stream of blue light that shone from above.

"I guess," she whispered. She looked up at the half-moon, its rays of light making her eyes sparkle. Rain ran down the length of her pale face as she wiped it away with her cold fingers.

"Do you want to go back inside?" Thaddeus asked her, fearing that she did.

"No, I'm fine," she said.

"Good," he smiled. Then taking a step sideways, he inched closer towards her, their hands brushing together by their sides.

Winnie felt his touch, and she wasn't sure if it were deliberate or by chance. Either way, she didn't move and let the back of his hand brush against hers. Then looking at him, she said, "Is everything okay?"

"Why shouldn't it be?" he asked, not looking at her but up at the moon.

"It's just that you seemed...rattled back in the house," she said, trying to find the right words, when really she thought he had looked scared.

"I just needed some air," he said. "The wine went straight to my head and I've got some work to do tonight. I just need to be able to think straight, that's all."

They stood quietly together, the sound of the rain thrumming off the leaves in the trees was all she could hear. There were no voices in the wind tonight, and she laughed at herself for being so stupid. Then, glancing at Thaddeus, she could see that sadness had come over his face again. Even though she stood next to him, their hands brushing together, she couldn't help but see how lonely he really was. What must it have been like for him, up here all alone? He'd told her that he had become a virtual recluse and she didn't want to become the same. So tugging at his hand, she said, "Hey, how about you show me around tomorrow?"

"What, the house you mean?" he said, turning away from the moon.

"No, not the house," Winnie sighed. "Show me around St. Ives. There must be some really beautiful spots. I'd really love to see them."

"Not tomorrow," he said. "I'll be sleeping."

"Well can't you drag yourself out of bed for just a few hours..." she started.

"I can't," he said. "I need my rest. Anyway – like I've already told you, I much prefer the moonlight to the daylight."

"But don't you see? That's why you feel so lonely all the time," Winnie told him. "You spend all night locked away in this place, and during the day, you sleep. Perhaps if you got out some more, things wouldn't seem so bad. You might meet some new people, make some friends and..."

"I'm sorry, but I just can't," he told her.

"But why?" she persisted. "I'd love for you to show me around..."

"Not tomorrow," he said, looking at her. "But I will – someday soon."

"Okay," she gave in. "But you know, if you really want a new beginning, you need to find one. I don't think you'll find a new start hidden away, wherever it is you hide during the day."

"Perhaps not," he said thoughtfully, and he seemed to be staring into the black slithers of darkness, which separated the trees.

Feeling disappointed, Winnie shrugged and said, "I'm going back inside."

"No, don't go," he said, grabbing her hand again. Unlike the gentle tug Winnie had given his hand, Thaddeus entwined his fingers with hers, locking them together. "Stay a little longer."

"Why?" she whispered.

"Because you look beautiful in the moonlight," he said.

Winnie stared at him, and however much she liked to hear him say she was beautiful, she couldn't help but fear he was thinking of Frances again. So trying to pull her hand free of his, she said, "Please let go of my hand."

"Why?" he asked, still holding on.

"Because you're pretending I'm her again," she said. "This is where she used to come and stand, isn't it?"

"No, *Frances* never came out here and stood in the moonlight," he said, whispering Frances's name. "By the time we moved here, she was very sick. She could hardly sit upright, let alone stand. I promise you, that's not the reason you are standing here."

"Why then?" she asked, searching his eyes, desperate to see if he was lying to her.

"Because you look beautiful," he said again.

"I don't believe it," she whispered, and pulled her hand free.

"You don't believe it because you don't want to believe it," he told her. "You've spent too many years of your life listening to people telling you that you are no good, that you are worthless and ugly. Why do you believe them and not me? You keep telling me to start over. Perhaps you should try practicing what you preach."

It wasn't Winnie who finally walked away, but Thaddeus. He turned away and headed back towards the house. At the front door, he looked back, but Winnie couldn't be sure if he were looking at her, or having one last look into the shadows amongst the trees behind her.

Chapter Twenty-One

By the time they had finished eating the girl, she was nothing more than a bunch of bones. Since the murder of the girl and her baby, the fact that there was now a massive police hunt for the killers didn't even bother them. They had just killed again, and what little flesh remained covered the blood-drenched mattress in stringy lumps. The female armed away the blood from her lips, while the two males licked their hands clean. The poky house on the outskirts of St. Ives held nothing else of interest. They had taken what they'd come for. Again, it had all been so very easy, and the male wondered if the humans would ever learn. If only he could meet one that resisted him, a girl who would offer a challenge. He knew the feeding would be so much sweeter for it.

"Satisfied?" he asked the others as he turned to leave the room, glancing down one last time at the bed, just in case there was any flesh he might have missed on the stripped carcass.

"No, Claude," the female said, crossing the room to him.

He could tell her hunger had been sedated as the fire in her eyes had faded – a little. She ran a slender set of fingers down his cheek. Claude spied a small spot of flesh in the corner of her mouth, and he slowly licked it away with the tip of his tongue. She kissed him back.

"We should be gone already," the other male said, brushing past them and heading for the front door.

Claude pushed the female away, and she smiled at him. "Why is he so tense tonight?"

"You know why," Claude said, heading out of the room.

And Michelle did know why. It was Frances. Everything was always about Frances. Without looking back, Michelle left the room and the bony remains of the girl, which glistened in the moonlight that poured through the window.

Chapter Twenty-Two

Winnie woke with a start. She sat up in bed, her heart racing. Had she dreamt about Thaddeus again? She couldn't be sure. The dream seemed just out of reach inside her head. Winnie closed her eyes in an attempt to claw it back. She wanted to recapture whatever had caused her heart to race; not out of fear, but an excitement you might feel when being close to someone you were attracted to. However much she screwed her eyes shut, she couldn't quite see who it was that lingered in the fog of her mind.

Thinking of Thaddeus, she showered and dressed, not in one of those violet tops or black skirts, but the denims and sweater she felt more comfortable wearing. As she made her way downstairs, she wondered what she would do to fill her day until Thaddeus woke that evening. She knew the windows needed cleaning for sure, and seeing as he was paying her to keep the house tidy, she thought she would make a start on the window where she had sat at Thaddeus's request. Winnie reached the bottom of the stairs and turned towards the kitchen, needing a slice of toast and coffee before she started to do anything. Pushing open the kitchen door and wishing that Thaddeus had agreed to show her around St. Ives that day, she stopped short when she saw him standing at the kitchen table. Sunlight poured in through the dirty windows, causing what appeared to be a halo around his head and shoulders. He glanced up at her in the open doorway.

"Thaddeus?" Winnie gasped, not expecting to see him standing there. After he had walked away from her the night before, he'd disappeared upstairs and she hadn't expected to see him until dusk.

"Good morning, Winnie," he smiled back at her.

"I didn't expect you to be awake." Then glancing up at the clock above the cooker, she added, "It's only eight-thirty in the morning."

"It's such a beautiful day," he smiled at her, as he placed a flask and some croissants into a small wicker basket that sat on the kitchen table. "Besides, it's my way of saying sorry."

"Sorry for what?" she frowned.

"For being such a grouch last night," he started to explain. "I didn't mean to walk off. I thought about what you said, and you were right. I should get out more. Hiding away all day and not facing the world isn't going to help me." Then closing the lid on the basket, he picked it up and added, "And I would love to show you around. I thought we could have breakfast on the beach."

"Are you serious?" Winnie wanted to squeal with excitement, but she held it back.

He winked at her and said, "C'mon. I know this really pretty spot. You'll love it."

Thaddeus led Winnie through the crop of trees in front of the house and towards the narrow coastal path which led down to the shore. As they walked together, Winnie looked up at the pale winter sun, and Thaddeus had been right, for February it was a beautiful day. Too nice to be cleaning windows, she thought. More than that, Winnie was so happy that Thaddeus had decided not to spend the day locked in his room, but with her.

The path led down towards the cliff's edge, and as they neared it, the sound of the waves crashing against the rocks below boomed in their ears. A fresh breeze blew Winnie's auburn hair around her shoulders and face. She dragged her hair from her eyes with her free hand. With St. Ives behind them, Thaddeus steered Winnie along the path which now sloped downwards. Throwing Thaddeus a sideways glance, she realised she hadn't actually seen him in daylight, and his skin was pale, the light brown stubble that covered the lower half of his face looking like a shadow. Like her own, his messy hair waved to and fro in the salty breeze. Again, she couldn't help but think of how good-looking he was, and what a shame that he kept himself locked away. He was still so young and would have a lot to give. As she threw him the occasional glance, Winnie knew, if she were being honest with herself, that she was growing to like him, despite his odd ways. The little voice buried deep inside of her didn't want Winnie to admit that. The little voice didn't want Winnie having feelings for such a complex man. Men like that could be dangerous, the voice tried to warn her. As if twisting the dial on a radio, Winnie turned down the volume on that little voice.

The path led to a small, sandy shore which was shaped like a golden horseshoe and lay at the foot of the cliffs. The beach was desolate and seagulls squawked overhead. There was a small, grassy bank which was covered in long shoots of purple heather. The sea rushed up the shoreline in long, foamy waves. Thaddeus had been right; this place was beautiful, Winnie thought. Then, just on the other side of the cove, she noticed what appeared to be a cave in the side of the cliff face. The mouth of it looked dark and the rocks all around it were black and slick, worn smooth by years of waves crashing against them.

"Is that a cave?" she asked, pointing into the distance.

"Yes, but you can only reach it when the tide is out," he said. "But even then I wouldn't risk it. Could be dangerous."

"Dangerous?" Winnie asked.

"The tide can come in quicker than you think," he explained. "You could get trapped. That cave fills up pretty good with water and you could drown." Then changing the subject, he said, "Let's take our shoes off or they'll get wet."

They took off their socks and trainers, and snatching them up with the basket, Thaddeus placed them out of the reach of the waves and on the grassy bank. Winnie watched as he pulled the black turtleneck top he was wearing from over his head and threw it down next to their shoes. Then rolling up the bottoms of his jeans, he ran into the sea.

"C'mon, Winnie!" he called out to her, splashing water with his hands.

"It's cold," she yelped, as the waves crashed over her toes.

"Aww, don't be such a baby!" he laughed.

So pulling the sweater from over her head to reveal a little black vest, and rolling up her jeans, she tiptoed into the water. "It's freezing!" she cried, wading towards him, arms wrapped around herself to keep warm.

"It's not cold," he grinned, spraying her with water.

"Thaddeus!" she shrieked, the water covering her. "Right! So that's how you want to play it!"

With her hands trailing in the sea, she splashed him with a wave of water. It covered him completely and he stood looking at her with water running through his hair, down his face, and over his naked chest.

"Look what you've done!" he laughed, running his long fingers through his hair. "I'm soaked. Right – now you're in for it!"

"No!" Winnie squealed as she waded away from him as fast as she could, back towards the shore. She wasn't quick enough, and she felt icy cold droplets of water soak her back. Winnie reached the shore, and with the sand seeping through her toes, she snatched up her sweater and ran towards the grass.

Thaddeus was right behind her, his hands cupped together, brimming with seawater. She turned, and doing so, she tripped over the wicker basket and fell into the grass. Rolling onto her back, she looked up to find Thaddeus towering over her, seawater dripping from between his fingers.

"Don't you dare!" she warned him, a smile on her lips.

"You should never dare me," he laughed, and splashed her with the water.

Winnie waved her hands out in an attempt to bat away as much of the freezing cold water as possible, but just as Thaddeus had intended, she got soaked. Sitting up in the grass, with her vest clinging to her and her hair wet and bedraggled-looking, Winnie stared up at Thaddeus and said, "Are you happy now? I'm freezing cold and wet."

"Come here," he said, dropping to his knees. "I'll warm you up."

"No, it's okay," she smiled, putting on her sweater. "I'm fine."

"I just don't want you to catch a cold. After all, it was me who covered you in water," Thaddeus said.

"Thanks, but I know how to look after myself," she smiled.

"You don't have to be so defensive," Thaddeus said. "I wasn't trying to get it on with you or anything like that."

"I'm not being defensive," she said. "It's just the way I am."

"Which is defensive," he smiled.

"I just don't want to get too close to anyone." And she looked away.

Sitting down beside her in the sand, Thaddeus said, "Is being friends too close for you?"

"No, friendship is just fine," she said, turning to face him again.

A length of her hair blew across her face, and Thaddeus reached out with his hand to brush it away, then stopped himself.

"It's okay," she smiled, as if giving him permission.

Slowly, Thaddeus brushed the length of hair from her eyes.

"Thank you," she whispered, gingerly taking his hand in hers.

Thaddeus looked down at her hand, which was now holding his. He then looked back at her and said, "Friends?"

"I think we both need a friend," she smiled. In her heart, she knew she had to stop being so defensive. Winnie knew that in a different time or place, she would have perhaps wanted more than just friendship from Thaddeus.

"Being friends seems like a good place to start," he said, looking at her. Like Winnie, he knew if given a different set of circumstances, he would have wanted more than just friendship from her, too.

Slowly, letting his hand slide from hers, Thaddeus unpacked the picnic basket. Together they ate breakfast as they sat and watched the waves crash against the shore.

As Winnie helped Thaddeus pack the flask and their empty plates into the wicker basket, she said, "What shall we do together this afternoon?"

With a look of regret on his face, Thaddeus said, "I'm sorry, Winnie, but I need to go home and pack."

"Pack?" Winnie asked, standing up. "Are you going somewhere?"

"My publisher called this morning," he explained, without turning to look at her. "They need me to go back to London and sign a contract."

"How long will you be gone?"

"Just tonight," Thaddeus said. "I'll be back tomorrow evening."

Winnie looked at him as he wedged his feet into his trainers. "Can I come with you?" she asked him.

Then, picking up the wicker basket, he looked at her and said, "Sorry, Winnie, but I need to go alone; perhaps next time."

"Okay," Winnie said with a shrug of her shoulders, as if it didn't matter to her either way.

Thaddeus walked up the beach towards the path, and Winnie followed. They walked in silence, both lost to their own thoughts. As they reached the house, Thaddeus paused at the front door and looked at Winnie. "Can you do just one thing for me tonight when I'm gone?" he asked her.

"What's that?"

"Come out here and stand in the moonlight," he said.

"Why?"

"Because it will be a full moon tonight," he half-smiled. "And you will look so beautiful in its light."

Not saying another word, Thaddeus stepped inside the house, where he packed for London.

Chapter Twenty-Three

Alone in the giant house, Winnie stood at the dirty window and watched Thaddeus make his way through the crop of trees and disappear from view. She turned away and moved from the lounge, to the kitchen, to the dining room, and back to the lounge again. She had taken Thaddeus's iPod from the dock in the kitchen, and trying to drown out the feelings of loneliness she now felt being in the giant house all alone, she listened to *The One That Got Away* by Katy Perry, over and over again.

Winnie thought back to the beach that morning, and she knew in her heart she had enjoyed being with Thaddeus. As she now wandered aimlessly about his huge home, there was a small part of her that wished he hadn't had to go to London. She would have really liked them to have spent the rest of the day together. Winnie wondered if Thaddeus had felt the same. The little voice inside her was telling her yes – Thaddeus had felt the same but only because Winnie reminded him of Frances. So Winnie turned up the volume on the iPod to drown that little voice out.

Perhaps Thaddeus was telling the truth when he said he just wanted to be friends? But would he ever want more than that? Maybe if she dropped her guard a little, she might find out. Feeling like she wanted to scream, and knowing she had to stop thinking about him or go insane, Winnie went to the kitchen. From the cupboard beneath the sink, she took a bucket and cloth, and filled it with warm, soapy water and went outside. It was late afternoon and the temperature had dropped. Placing the bucket on the ground, she went back into the house and took the coat with the grey hood from the hook. With it buttoned up the front and the hood on, she went back outside. She went around the side of the house to the kitchen window. Here she scrubbed away the dirt and the grime which was smeared over the windows. How had they gotten so dirty? Trying desperately not to think of Thaddeus, she scrubbed until the water was a muddy brown in colour and was cold. With her hands looking like two lumps of raw meat, she went back into the kitchen where she refilled the bucket.

Outside again, she noticed that the sunlight had almost faded away for the day, and it had grown almost dark. Not wanting to go back into the house and listen to those voices of doubt inside her head, she went to the window where she had sat the night before, wearing Frances's clothes, and reading the book that Thaddeus had left out for her. She would rather carry on working in the dark; she had all night to listen to her own self-doubts. She would rather keep busy.

With the light fading fast, she placed the bucket on the ground and took the cloth from the water. It was then that Winnie noticed something she thought to be strange. With the sodden cloth turning cold in her hands, she knelt down and inspected the flowerbed beneath the window. The heads of the flowers looked as if they had been trampled flat. Winnie brushed some of them aside, and frowned at the footprints she could clearly see in the earth. Who would have been standing in the flowerbed, and why? What could be the reason? Then, looking down at the footprints again, then back at the window, her skin turned cold. Somebody had been standing in the flowerbed so they could spy through the window and into the room. The window was so filthy that whoever had been spying through it would have had to stand in the flowerbeds to get a half-decent view of what lay on the other side. Winnie stepped into the footprints and looked through the window. Peering through the dirt smeared across it, she could just make out the chair where she had sat reading the night before, dressed as Frances.

With her heart starting to pound in her chest, she remembered how Thaddeus had been talking, and she had caught him glancing up at the window. Had he seen someone there? Her heart sped up.

"The kitchen window," she whispered aloud, remembering how she had thought Thaddeus had been looking at someone or something the night before. Picking up the bucket of water, she stepped away from the window, her heart and mind racing. Then, with gooseflesh crawling up her back, she remembered how in the Light House Restaurant, Thaddeus had insisted that she sat with her back to the window. There, too, she had caught him glancing over her shoulder and out of the window, as if someone had been there. Had someone been watching Thaddeus? Had someone been watching *her*, she suddenly thought, and dropped the bucket.

While Winnie had been trying to figure out what the footprints meant, and if either she or Thaddeus had been spied on, the moon had gradually risen in the night sky behind her. She looked up into the star-shot sky. Thaddeus had been right; the moon was full and round and shining brightly down at her.

Stand in the moonlight, she heard him ask her, as if he was breathing in her ear. Winnie spun around at the sound of rustling beneath the trees. She peered into the darkness, but could see nothing. Guessing she was just spooking herself, she turned back to face the window and screamed. Reflected in it, and staring out of the dark from beneath the trees, were those three pale faces.

Chapter Twenty-Four

Winnie stumbled out of the pool of moonlight and back towards the house. The bucket she had dropped rolled behind her, and she fell backwards and onto the ground. Air exploded from her lungs, and she felt as if she had been punched. Without taking her eyes off the three faces staring back at her from the darkness, she dragged herself to her feet.

"You don't have to be scared," one of the faces whispered, its voice seeming to float on the air towards her.

On her feet again, Winnie screwed up her eyes and peered into the darkness. The face spoke again and said, "You know you don't have to fear us. It's Thaddeus you should be scared of."

The voice sounded male as it floated towards Winnie.

"What do you want?" she called out, her heart in her throat.

"What we've always wanted," the voice said back.

"And what's that?" Winnie trembled, inching her way backwards towards the open front door, not daring to take her eyes away from the faces for one moment.

"For you to come with us," the voice said again. "It's only going to be a matter of time before he kills you, Frances. You know it to be true."

"What did you call me?" Winnie whispered, reaching the open front door and stepping backwards through it.

"Frances, stop these games," the voice said again, the face as bright and as white as the moon.

"I'm not Frances." Winnie shook, her fingers curling around the frame of the front door, readying herself to close it.

"What did you say?" the voice asked, and it sounded as if it were growing angry.

"Frances is dead," Winnie shivered, pulling back her hood.

As if what she had said had caused the face beneath the tree great anguish, it released a gut-wrenching scream, so loud that the windows rattled in their frames. Winnie threw her hands over her ears, and screwed her eyes shut. Within an instant, the screaming had stopped, and she snapped open her eyes to see the three faces were standing before her at the door. They weren't just faces. They had bodies, too, which were clad in black clothing. Two of them were male, the other female. The first was thin and tall, with black hair that was swept back off his brow. The second male was just as tall, but thicker set, with short, cropped, black hair. The female had hair which was dark blue, and blustered about her shoulders in the wind. Just like the other two, she wore a long, black coat, tight black denims, and boots. Although Winnie was scared of them, she couldn't help but be momentarily stunned by their striking beauty. The three of them, as they stood motionless before the door, looked immaculate. Their pale skin seemed almost translucent in the moonlight, and their crystal-clear blue eyes shone from their faces.

"What do you want?" Winnie breathed.

"Frances," the thin one hissed, just inches from her face.

"Frances died," Winnie mumbled.

"I don't believe it," he roared, his face now cast into an agonising grimace. "Tell me it's not true!"

The other two drew closer to the male who wailed as if in pain. They looked at Winnie.

"Invite us in so we can see for ourselves" the female said, her beautiful mouth curling upwards into a smile.

"No," Winnie snapped, closing the door.

Before it had locked, the door was forced open again, sending Winnie sprawling backwards onto her arse. She looked up and the three strangers, with their deathly white faces, crowded together just outside the doorway.

"Just invite us in so we can see if you are lying about Frances," the female smiled. "We won't hurt you."

From her position on the hallway floor, it looked to Winnie as if the beautiful woman's legs went on forever. However much the female smiled down at her, Winnie could see a cruelty in her eyes. She looked at the male, whose face was contorted with grief.

"Frances!" he screeched over and over again, tearing at his clothes as if trying to free himself from them. The other male tried to restrain him in his fit of madness. "Leave me, Claude!" the male screamed as if in agony.

"Nate, we don't know that Frances is dead," the female said.

"She is *dead*," he screamed. "I feel it in my blood. I know it to be true. He has murdered her." Again, he tore at his clothes with his hands, as if he were burning alive beneath them.

The female went to him, and lashing out at her, he pushed her away. "Leave me, Michelle. Don't touch me. I am in agony!" Then he stared down into the hallway, where Winnie looked on, her heart racing inside of her. The male called Nate then screamed at her, beating his chest with his fists in anguish. "Is this how I am repaid for letting him live? Her father was a fool to have put his faith in him!"

Winnie trembled uncontrollably. She couldn't remember feeling so scared. Her legs felt like rubber as she tried to stand, the male screeching, hissing, and spitting at her from the doorway. Holding onto the wall for support, she hobbled towards the open door. However much the male cast out his threats, she sensed that unless she invited them into the house, they could not enter, although she couldn't figure out why. Praying she was right, she inched towards them.

"My beloved Frances is burning in Hell, and so shall he!" he screamed at her, spit flying from his lips, and his eyes bulging with tears. "You, too, will die for what has happened here. I will avenge her death. I will not stop until I have drained both of you of your blood!"

Unable to bear his threats and the screeching of his voice any longer, Winnie threw herself at the door and forced it shut. With her back against it, she slid to the floor as quickly as the tears now spilt down her face. With the sound of the male's screams of grief burning in her ears, Winnie crawled away from the door on her hands and knees. Her body shuddered as she desperately fought to control her sobbing. The front door rattled in its frame, as the strangers outside threw themselves against it. The banging and thudding was so loud, Winnie feared it was going to explode off its hinges and into the hallway. Scrambling to her feet, and the sounds of her petrified sobs almost as loud as the door crashing in its frame, Winnie made her way into the lounge and then screamed.

The female was at the window, the one Winnie had recently cleaned. The tip of her nose was pressed against it as she screamed through the glass at Winnie. *"Let us in! You must let us in!"*

With her hands over her ears, Winnie made her way to the window. She quickly made sure it was locked, then pulled the curtains shut over the beautiful white face that glared in at her.

"Thaddeus!" Winnie screamed until her throat felt raw. The sound of her cries seemed to excite those outside, as they began banging on the windows.

"Let us in!" they screeched.

The lounge was now in darkness as Winnie tripped and stumbled towards the hallway. The little voice inside of her was screaming for her to get help. From where? Winnie knew she was miles from anywhere, and the only person who did know she was in the house was Thaddeus.

Do you have any family? She heard Thaddeus whisper in her ear, as she thought of their first meeting and how he had questioned her. The sudden realisation that perhaps he had somehow deceived her, made Winnie want to vomit. Doubting that she could rely on Thaddeus to come and save her, she desperately tried to think of how she was going to get away from those who screeched and banged on the windows outside. Even if Thaddeus could somehow know the danger she was now in, he was hundreds of miles away in London.

*My publisher telephoned this morning...*Winnie heard him say.

"Telephone!" Winnie cried out. She couldn't remember seeing one anywhere since arriving at the house. There must be one, Winnie's frantic mind tried to reason. She hadn't noticed Thaddeus in possession of a mobile phone, either. There must be a phone somewhere – how did he take the call from his publisher?

In the dark, and with the sound of the strangers outside banging against the door and the windows, Winnie raced into the dining room. With her hands outstretched before her, she searched for a telephone in the dark. With her heart slamming in her chest, and fighting hard to draw breath, she went back to the hall and climbed the stairs, passing the pictures that sat silently staring at each other. Winnie staggered along the landing, trying the handle of each door that she passed. All of them were locked. Then from above she heard a scratching noise, as if those people had somehow managed to climb up the side of the house and were now scrambling across the roof. Winnie shoulder-barged into each of the locked doors until the pain in her arm became too much too bear.

With the sound of scratching and clawing from above, Winnie raced along the landing to her room. Pushing open the door, she fell onto the floor in a heap. She cried out. Then the banging came again, and she looked up to see the female, Michelle, perched on the window ledge just outside her room. With her thick, blue hair billowing out behind her like a fan, Michelle tapped on the window with a set of long, black fingernails.

"Invite me in," she whispered against the window. *"Go on, you know you want to."*

"Leave me alone!" Winnie cried out, dragging herself to her feet and pulling the curtains shut.

Even though Winnie could no longer see her, she knew the woman was still there. Winnie knew they were all out there by the sounds of their tapping against the window, and the noise of them scrambling overhead. On her hands and knees, Winnie crawled over to her bed, where she pulled herself up onto it. As if to make herself as small as possible, Winnie drew her knees up to her chest. She pulled the hood of the coat over her head, and shut her eyes. Rocking slowly back and forth, she tried to block out the sounds of those strangers with the pale faces knocking at the window, screaming to be invited in.

Chapter Twenty-Five

Winnie had no idea how long she lay in the dark, trying to block out the sounds of those strangers outside. With her eyes shut tight, and cradling herself in the foetal position on the bed, Winnie prayed for them to go away. How had they got up to her bedroom window? How could they possibly be scampering over the roof? Perhaps they had climbed up the wild ivy that covered the front of the house? She tried to reason with herself, but the little voice inside of her doubted that. Just like everything else in life that seemed inexplicable, people always tried to find an explanation.

And when would Thaddeus be back? She wanted him to return. In her head, fused with the screeching and banging coming from outside in the dark, Winnie could hear Nate's voice. She remembered him screeching that 'HE' had murdered Frances. Was 'HE' Thaddeus? She feared it to be true. Thaddeus had told her Frances had died almost a year ago of cancer. If Frances truly had died that way, why, then, had Nate been screaming that he would not rest until he had avenged her death? As she rocked back and forth in fear, it was only then, as she fought to try and make sense of everything she had seen and heard, that she realised the tapping at the windows and scrambling sounds from above had stopped.

Winnie lay dead still. She dared not to even blink. Perhaps they had gone away – given up, realising that she would never let them in. With her eyes still closed, she listened for the slightest sound, the smallest of movements, but all she could hear was the sound of her heart racing and the wind blowing about the eaves. Again, she did not know how long she stayed there like that, focusing on the slightest creak, on the whispering of the leaves of the trees outside as they rustled in the wind. Eventually, believing that perhaps they had indeed gone – for now at least – Winnie pulled the hood from over her head, opened her eyes, and peered into the darkness of her room. Slices of moonlight shone from around the edges of the curtains covering her window, and she could just make out the shape of the dressing table and closets in the corner. Taking small, shallow breaths, Winnie climbed from her bed. She stood like a statue in the middle of her room, again listening for the slightest of sounds. When she was satisfied that she couldn't hear the strangers, she crept slowly towards the window.

With her body shaking and trembling, Winnie slowly reached out and gripped the edge of the curtain. She waited, making sure that she couldn't hear them, but the only noise came from the groaning wind outside. Then, very slowly, Winnie peeled back the edge of the curtain, like a nurse carefully removing the dressing from an infected wound. With her eye pressed close to the gap she had made, she peered out into the night. The moon shone high above her, casting its milky-blue rays over everything in its sight. Winnie dared to glance down, and then left and right, but she couldn't see any sign of the strangers. She let the curtain fall slowly back into place.

Standing alone in the middle of her room, the temptation to bolt down the stairs, throw open the door, and run for her life was overwhelming. Dare she risk it? Her scrambled mind tried to reason this. What if they were still out there? Winnie knew she was miles from town, from the nearest house – from anyone who might be able to help her. Wouldn't it be safer to stay locked in the house? They couldn't get in or they already would have, she told herself. Was she really going to wait for Thaddeus to arrive home? The little voice in her spoke up. What if he was a part of all of this somehow? What if he really had murdered Frances? Then she thought of the bedroom Thaddeus had discovered her in, the room with the sewing machine, the narrow bed, and the boarded-up windows. Why had he boarded them over? Was Frances's body hidden in there somewhere, perhaps beneath the bed, bloated, and being eaten by maggots?

With that terrifying image seesawing before her, Winnie raced across her room and yanked open the door, just wanting to be free of the house – of Thaddeus. Almost blind with fear and the darkness on the landing outside her room, Winnie ran towards the top of the wide staircase. Her legs felt like she was wading through the sea again. Each step slow and sluggish. Winnie stumbled past the room with the boarded-up windows, and the sight of those photographs of the ancient lady flashed before her mind.

"...*was she your grandmother?*" she heard herself ask Thaddeus.

"...*yes,*" he had smiled at her.

And as Winnie stared at the door, the sound of her breathing now more like a shallow rasp as her chest rose up and down, she remembered the night she had first met Thaddeus. He had said he didn't have any family. Thaddeus had told her he was all alone.

But not anymore, the little voice inside Winnie was now screaming.

"*Thaddeus isn't alone anymore, Winnie, because he has you,*" the little voice said. This time the little voice didn't sound as if it had come from within her...but behind her.

With her eyes wide open with fear, Winnie slowly turned her head and looked back into the darkness behind her. She had left her door open and a stream of moonlight poured out onto the landing. With arms and legs shaking beyond control, and streams of tears running the length of her face, Winnie looked at the little girl standing in the moonlight. Her red coat almost glistened as much as the stream of vomit, which snaked from the corner of her mouth.

"Ruby?" Winnie sobbed.

"Why haven't you been listening to me?" Ruby whispered. "I've been trying to tell you that you are in danger. Why haven't you been listening to that little voice inside of you?"

"But you died..." Winnie choked on her tears, feeling as if she were going to suffocate. "You shouldn't be here..."

"*Run! Run! RUN!*" the little girl standing in the moonlight screamed at Winnie.

Spinning around, Winnie did what she had always done, and ran. At the top of the stairs, Winnie looked back over her shoulder, but there was no sign of the pool of moonlight, or her friend, Ruby Little. Feeling as if she were somehow going insane, Winnie turned and raced down the stairs and into the hallway. In her fear and desperation to get away, she threw open the front door and screamed.

"Please invite us in," Nate grinned, his mouth stretching across his face.

Chapter Twenty-Six

Winnie slammed the door shut with such force, it rattled in its frame. She pressed her back against it. At once, the strangers outside began to pound against the door with their fists. There was another sound, too, which Winnie could now hear. It sounded like claws being dragged down the windowpane in the lounge. It was ear-splitting and Winnie threw her hands over her ears.

"Leave me alone!" she screamed, hot tears blinding her.

The desperation and sheer terror in her voice excited the strangers outside, and they threw themselves against the door. Winnie rocked forward under the weight of them crashing against it.

"This could all be over," one of them hissed, "You know what you have to do."

"Never!" Winnie sobbed, crawling away from the door on her stomach, sliding like a snake into the lounge. Looking up, she could see the silhouette of one them dragging their fingernails down the length of the window.

"Please," the silhouette hissed.

Winnie recognised the voice to be that of the woman, Michelle.

When Michelle got no answer from Winnie, she began to tap lightly on the glass, as if teasing her somehow. "It's not you we want," Michelle said from outside, her voice sounding softer now. "We just want Thaddeus."

"He's not here," Winnie cried out.

"You lie!" came the voice of Nate from behind the front door. "And I will *burn* you for it."

"He's not here!" Winnie screamed.

"Let us take a look for ourselves." This time it was the voice of Claude she could hear, as if coming from above her – the roof, perhaps.

"No," Winnie sobbed into the balls of her hands. "No, I can't let you in."

"Yes, you can," Michelle said, her voice soothing now, like an older sister trying to offer some understanding and comfort. "We won't hurt you. It's Thaddeus we want."

With the sound of Michelle's fingernails tapping against the window quickening, and the banging on the door growing louder again, Winnie felt as if she were being mentally tortured. She felt as if her mind was being chipped away at, and bit by bit, her resolve, her strength to defy the strangers outside was being broken down.

"Just ask us to come in," Michelle whispered. "You don't even have to stay. You could take the chance to run. To get far away from Thaddeus. He is the one who will kill you, not us."

With Michelle's words floating around in her mind, and knowing that she just wanted to run and run until her heart burst, Winnie pulled herself to her feet and walked slowly towards the front door.

"You promise you won't hurt me?" she sobbed, her arm shaking uncontrollably as she reached out for the door handle. "You promise you will let me run far away from here?"

"We promise," Nate said, his voice now sounding as smooth as silk, like Michelle's.

With her heart beating at a deafening level in her ears, Winnie curled her fingers around the door handle. Then, in between the beats of her heart, she heard another sound. A voice – a *little* voice.

No, it whispered.

Winnie snapped her head around, half expecting to see her friend, Ruby Little, standing at the foot of the stairs, bathed in moonlight, her bright red coat shining, like the drool of vomit encrusted around her mouth. There was no moonlight, and no Ruby Little. Winnie looked down at her fingers curled around the door handle, then let them slowly slip away.

"I won't invite you in," she whispered, closing her eyes.

No sooner had the words passed over her lips, the strangers outside erupted in a frenzy of anger.

"I will burn you," Nate hissed around the edges of the doorframe. "I will *burn* both of you."

With her back against the wall in the hallway, Winnie slid slowly to the floor. She sat in the dark, listening to the strangers' threats, then promises, and pleas. With her eyes shut tight, and hands pressed flat against her ears, she thought of her friend, Ruby Little, as if waiting to hear her tiny voice again. It didn't come. Just before dawn, the banging and the screeching from the other side of the front door finally stopped. Winnie was unaware that it had, as she had finally given in to her tiredness, and fell asleep on the hallway floor.

Chapter Twenty-Seven

Why did you clean the windows? the voice asked.

The voice came again, but Winnie just thought it was coming from somewhere way off in her dream. She felt cold. The surface beneath her was too hard to be the wild heather and grass she was lying on in her dream.

Why did you clean the dirt from the windows? the voice came again, and Winnie recognised it to be Thaddeus's.

She rolled over to find him lying next to her. Winnie could hear the sound of the sea rushing up the shore. The sun was high above her, and its bright rays of light blurred her view of him. She could see his chest was bare. She feared that he was still in love with Frances, the woman he had once loved...the woman he had murdered.

Why did you clean the windows? she heard him ask yet again behind the dazzling sunlight.

Because it's my job, she whispered, suddenly feeling scared. *Because if I didn't clean the windows, you would be angry with me. You would murder me just like you murdered...*

"...Frances," Winnie murmured, opening her eyes. She looked up to see Thaddeus standing over her.

"What did you say?" he asked, a deep frown across his brow.

"Huh?" she mumbled, rubbing sleep from her eyes.

"Why did you clean the dirt off the windows?" he repeated, reaching down and pulling Winnie to her feet.

"What?" Winnie flustered, feeling disorientated and thick-headed. She slowly glanced about as if getting her bearings, and she could see by the pale light that was streaming through the open front door, that it was dusk. How long had she slept? She wondered. Then focusing on the front door again, she pulled herself free of Thaddeus's grasp, ran across the hall and slammed it shut.

With a perplexed look on his face, and seeing the sudden look of fear in her eyes, Thaddeus said, "What's wrong?"

Winnie turned to face him, and as the memories of what had happened the night before flooded her mind, she turned around and yanked open the front door again. Before she had even stepped over the threshold, Thaddeus had taken hold of her arm again.

"Get the fuck off me!" she screamed at him, punching and kicking out wildly at him.

· "What's wrong?" he said, soaking up her punches.

"You're a freaking murderer, that's what's wrong!" she yelled at him.

Looking as if he had been suddenly struck across his face, Thaddeus said, "What are you talking about? Who has said this about me?"

"The faces I saw in the moonlight!" she shouted, trying to pull free of him. "The faces you said I had imagined."

"Did they speak to you?" he snapped. Then shaking her like a ragdoll, he roared, "What did you tell them? What did they say?"

Winnie looked into his eyes and screamed, *"Apart from wanting to rip your fucking heart out, and drain you of all your blood, they said you murdered Frances."*

Hearing this, Thaddeus glanced back at the tree line, and then slamming the door shut, he paced up and down the hallway. Thaddeus ran his long fingers through his hair. He looked anxious and drawn. Then turning, he stared at Winnie and said, "Oh my God, what have I done? I've failed."

"Did you kill Frances?" Winnie yelled, screwing her hands into fists by her sides.

Then, taking a step closer to her, he whispered, "Yes, I killed her."

Chapter Twenty-Eight

Winnie reached for the door handle again, but Thaddeus was too quick and gripped her wrist.

"It's not what you think," he shouted at her, his eyes dark and desperate-looking. "Yes I killed her, but it was an accident. I never meant to kill her."

"You said she died of cancer," Winnie spat at him.

"I didn't murder her!" he shouted, the veins bulging beneath the flesh that covered his neck. *"You've got to believe me."*

"Why should I believe a word you say?" she yelled back. "You've done nothing but lie to me since I arrived here! I should never have accepted your offer. I should've stayed in London. By the sounds of it, I would have been safer living and sleeping on the streets."

Winnie turned her back on him and opened the front door.

"Where are you going?" he asked her.

"Back where I came from," she said. "Back to what I know."

"You can't leave," he whispered over her shoulder.

Winnie could feel him behind her, his breath cold against the nape of her neck. "Why not?" she breathed, too scared to turn around.

"Because it's almost dark outside and they will be back before you reach the end of the coastal path," he said.

"What? These people you've pissed off only come out at night, do they?" she asked with a sneer.

"They aren't people," Thaddeus whispered in her ear. "They are vampires."

With the sound of disbelief in her voice, Winnie said, "Bullshit. There isn't any such thing as vampires."

"Nor werewolves?" he said, pulling her around to face him.

With her eyes wide open, and a scream trying to escape from her throat, Winnie collapsed in shock against the door.

Dropping to her knees, she fought desperately to suck air into her lungs as she looked up at him. Thaddeus stood before her, his eyes bright and yellow, like two burning suns. The shape of his face hadn't changed. He still looked like Thaddeus, other than the bushy-looking sideburns which now covered his cheeks. His hands had changed, Winnie noticed, as she stared in horror at him. Where he had once had those long, slender fingers, were now a huge set of claws. They looked strong and powerful – deadly.

"What the fuck is going on here?" Winnie finally gasped. "What are you?"

"I am a Lycanthrope," he said, baring a set of razor-sharp-looking teeth. "But you would probably know me better by the more common term, werewolf, or wolf man."

"You're not real," Winnie gasped. "None of this is real. *Things* like you are just stuff off stories and nightmares."

Thaddeus took one of her hands in his claws. She immediately tried to pull away, but he held firm. His claws felt warm. The skin covering them was coarse and tough. Then, taking her hand, he placed it against his chest. Beneath his fine cotton shirt, she could feel his heart racing.

"I'm very real and so are the vampires you say came here last night," he whispered.

"Are you going to kill me like you killed Frances?" Winnie breathed.

"If my reasons for bringing you here were to simply kill you, I would have done so already," he said, letting go of her hand.

"So why did you bring me here?" Winnie asked, pressing herself against the door, desperate to keep as much distance between her and Thaddeus as possible.

He saw her flinch away, and desperate to show Winnie she had nothing to fear from him, he walked over to the staircase and sat on the bottom stair. Then, looking over at her as she cowered in the darkening shadows, he said, "As you can see, vampires and werewolves are very real. We don't make the habit of revealing ourselves. The reaction that you've just had is proof enough that we are better off living in secret, keeping ourselves away from humans as much as possible. They would only hunt us down and kill us. We have done that to our own species well enough without the help of humans."

"What's that supposed to mean?" Winnie asked, drawing her knees up beneath her chin.

"I am the last of my race," he started to explain. "Hundreds of years ago, our two races inhabited the Carpathian Mountains, which bordered the countries of Bukovina and Moldavia. For as long as we lived in those mountains, the vampires and Lycanthrope fought for dominance of the region. The vampires were far greater in number, and they hunted down and killed my race. They drove us to the very brink of extinction. With only a small pack of us left, we fled the mountains, but this wasn't enough for the vampires, they wanted all of us dead. They pursued us across the remote regions of Eastern Europe. One by one, they killed the Lycanthrope until there was only the one left – *me*," he said, patting his chest with his claw.

"I managed to outwit them and stay alive, which enraged Nicodemus, the pale king of the vampire race. So desperate to hang my dead body from the walls which surrounded his castle high up in Carpathian Mountains, he sent his most cunning and ruthless warrior to hunt me down and kill me. For months, this feared warrior tracked me down, until at last, I was ensnared. But Nicodemus's plan went wrong, because instead of killing me, Nicodemus's most deadly warrior fell in love with me. Not only had he lost a great warrior, but he had lost his daughter, Frances, as it was she who he sent to kill me. Nicodemus had promised his daughter's heart to his second most trusted. A vampire by the name of Nate Varna."

"He was one of those staring at me from beneath the trees," Winnie said.

"I know," Thaddeus said, looking at her with his yellow eyes.

"You knew all along," Winnie said, feeling betrayed by Thaddeus.

"Yes," he said with a nod of his head. "When Nate Varna discovered that the woman he loved – the woman who had been promised to him – had given her heart to a werewolf, he became lost in a fit of rage and despair. He vowed to Nicodemus that he would hunt me down and not only bring my carcass back, but his daughter, too, where she rightfully belonged. Frances heard of Nate's plan, so in secret, she visited her father and told him that if I were ever to be killed, she would take her own life, too. Loving his daughter with all his heart, and not wanting to be responsible for Frances taking her own life, he forbid Nate from pursuing us. However much Nicodemus detested and loathed the thought of his daughter being in love with a Lycanthrope, he hated the thought of her killing herself even more.

"But Nate was restless, believing I would one day kill Frances, murder her as she slept, to avenge the death of my race. Knowing what Nate feared could happen to his daughter, a deal was struck. It was agreed that once every year, Frances would stand beneath the light of a full moon, so Nate could look upon the woman that he had lost to a werewolf. The night of a full moon was chosen, as on that night I would be safely locked away during my change, so that I couldn't hurt Frances. Although the agreement stated that Nate was never to approach or speak to Frances, but only to look at her from afar, he could take comfort in the fact, that those precious moments were just his and not shared by me.

"For hundreds of years the agreement was kept and Frances and I shared a wonderful life together. However, some fifty years ago, Frances became distressed by the thought of having to parade herself beneath the moonlight. It had become like a millstone around her neck, and she feared she would never be free of Nate Varna. So we would move around from one country to the next, as there was nothing in the agreement stating we couldn't do so. More often than not, Nate and those he travelled with would track us down. Some years they were unable to find us, but mostly they did. I would read the foreign newspapers searching for any articles about the brutal deaths of young women, as everywhere they went, they left death behind them. In that way, I could keep a track of them, like they kept a track of me and Frances.

"Although she couldn't see Nate, as he was never to reveal himself to her; Frances felt he was somehow inching closer to her as the years passed by – closer than the agreement allowed. On the very last occasion that Frances stood beneath the moonlight, she was convinced that she could hear him calling to her on the wind, begging her to leave me and go with him. So we packed up our possessions and moved again. This time, to France. Both of us were fluent in speaking French, so we hired a maid, and before long, we had set up a new home and started yet another new life for ourselves. Being a vampire, Frances had to sleep during the day and live by night. I didn't have to, but I chose to so we could be together. Frances needed to drink blood to survive, but not necessarily the blood of humans, she could survive just as well on the blood from deer and other such animals. Only vampires who enjoy the thrill of killing humans need their blood. I, however, change every full moon into a wolf," he said.

"I can see that," Winnie murmured looking across the darkening hallway at him.

"No, this is not me as a full wolf," he smiled, showing his pointed teeth. "I can choose to look like this anytime I want to, full moon or not. During the night of a full moon, I change into my true form, that of a giant wolf - *hound* - whatever people choose to call me. It's while in that form I am unable to have rational thoughts. I become nothing more than a wild animal, unable to think or reason. I act purely on instinct and the desire to hunt and kill. Therefore, Frances would lock me away on the night of a full moon, and release me the following day. As a wolf I do not discriminate between victims. I would've happily ripped her throat out as that of another."

"But you did end up killing her though, didn't you?" Winnie asked him.

Thaddeus lowered his head and looked at the floor, as if it brought him too much shame to say what happened next. "In France, there was a stone coalbunker at the far reaches of our land. The walls were thick and solid, made from giant slabs of stone. There was an iron door with a lock. It was an ideal place to contain me during my change," he explained. "So on the day of each full moon, I went out to the coalbunker where Frances would lock me inside. She kept the key with her always, never letting it out of her sight. It hung from a chain around her neck. While walking away from the coalbunker that day, she noticed the chain had broken, and placed the key into the pocket of her dress.

"Sometimes, as our maid served dinner, she would casually ask what it was we kept in the coalbunker and where could she find the key should she need it. Frances politely assured the maid that she would never need the key, and steered the conversation onto other matters. Frances forgot about the key in her pocket. That evening as the maid gathered together the dirty laundry, she discovered the key. So just before dawn the following morning, before waking Frances for her breakfast, the maid crept out to the coalbunker, and using the key she had found, she opened the door. I can't say I remember killing her, but hours later, I discovered her disembowelled remains strewn across the fields at the back of the house. I gathered together what was left of her half-eaten body and burnt her remains. She wasn't the only person I had given a death sentence to," he said, looking slowly up at Winnie.

"In my bloodthirsty rage, I had gone back to the house and crept up to the room I shared with Frances. I only recall brief fragments of what happened next, but Frances told me that she awakened to find me snarling at the foot of the bed. Not knowing how I had been set free, and fearing I would surely kill her, Frances desperately tried to shoo me away. As a wolf I would have smelt the fear reeking from her. I must have, as Frances later told me I lunged at her. She kicked out with her foot and I sunk my jaws into her ankle, snapping the bones as if they were nothing more than twigs. Dawn had just broken and the moon was fading, taking with it its power over me. So before I could attack Frances again, I began to change back into a man. I woke to discover Frances sobbing in pain upon the bed, and although she wasn't dead, we knew it was only a matter of time.

"A Lycanthrope bite to a vampire is fatal, even if it doesn't kill them outright," Thaddeus explained. "It is a slow and painful death, tearing away the hundreds of years they have lived. It is like age catches up with them, and they grow older in a matter of months, decaying away until they are nothing more than dust. So once bitten by me, both Frances and I knew she was going to die, fade away before my eyes. Frances didn't fear her own death, she feared mine. We knew that it was only a month or two before Nate would come again, expecting to see Frances standing in the moonlight, so he could satisfy himself that the woman he loved was still alive and well, and I hadn't killed her as he believed I would do. If Frances wasn't standing in the moonlight where we lived, he would know there was something wrong and come looking for me – to kill me.

"So we fled here, to England, just days before his arrival in France. With a full moon only days away, and Frances too sick and frail to lock me away, I had to find someplace where I could be kept from harming her or anyone else. It was then I discovered the cave which you pointed out on the beach yesterday morning," he said, staring at Winnie. "I would walk around the cove while the tide was out. At night it comes in, pulled by the force of the full moon. Here I could change, unable to get back to shore. The rocks surrounding it are far too smooth for me to scramble up. So I am trapped there until the moon fades at dawn and I change back."

"That's where you were last night, wasn't it?" Winnie asked him.

"Yes," he said. "I had to go there so as not to harm you – just like I harmed Frances."

"It was her in those pictures I found in that room upstairs," Winnie breathed, as some of what Thaddeus was explaining slotted into place. "She was the old woman in the photographs."

"Yes," Thaddeus said, the light behind his eyes fading. "She turned to dust in that room a year ago. Her remains looked just like ashes, so I took them down to the shore and set her free at last. I boarded the windows over as Frances became too weak to leave the room in the end, and she was in there day and night. I couldn't risk any daylight creeping in. So as you can see, Winnie, I did kill Frances, but not as you have been led to believe."

Winnie sat by the door, her knees still tucked beneath her chin as she tried to make sense of everything he had told her. She glanced up at the pictures hanging opposite each other on the walls. "So are those paintings of you and Frances?"

"Yes," he said, glancing up at them. "They span the three hundred years we spent together."

"So how old are you then, because you don't look a day over twenty-five," Winnie said.

"Thanks," Thaddeus half-smiled.

"It wasn't a compliment, dickhead," she snapped.

"Four-hundred and twenty-three, give or take a year or two," he said back.

They sat quietly, neither of them knowing what to say. Then when the silence became almost unbearable, Winnie looked at him and said, "You've used me."

"I know I have," he said, unable to bring himself to meet her stare. "It had been almost a year since Frances had died. I'd been searching those foreign newspapers for news stories about brutal deaths. I knew by the horrific stories I found that Nate and the other two, who sometimes travelled with him, were closing in. If they found me here, and Frances wasn't standing in the moonlight, they would suspect something had happened to her. If they discovered that she was dead, then my stay of execution would be over and the last of my race would be dead. I was called to London to meet with my publisher, that is true, but by chance I happened to see you one evening outside the tube station, as I've already explained. To look at you was like looking at Frances – it was uncanny. Those nights I sat looking at you, it wasn't because I wanted you to take Frances's place in my heart. I wanted you to take her place in the moonlight."

"You bastard," Winnie said, now truly understanding the level of Thaddeus's deceit.

"I was scared and desperate," Thaddeus tried to explain. "I thought that perhaps if you dressed in Frances's clothes and stood in the moonlight with the hood up, Nate would believe that he had seen Frances, and go away. That would have given me another year or perhaps more to escape, truly hide my tracks from the vampires forever. I remembered what Frances had told me, how she suspected Nate was watching her on more than just the night of the full moon. So I needed to be seen out with you. I needed him to see us together, happy, holding hands."

"That's why you took me out to that restaurant," Winnie suddenly gasped, feeling as if she had been punched in the stomach. "That's why you kept looking over my shoulder and out of the window. You were checking to see if he was out there, watching. So you made me sit with my back to the window just in case he was, so he believed he was looking at Frances, because we had the same colour hair."

"Yes," Thaddeus whispered, ashamed by what he had done. "I wasn't really mad about the fish fingers – in fact, I quite like them. I needed a reason to get you out and about at night, as Frances and I would have so often done. Then as we made our way back to the house, I noticed the moonlight. I wanted to see if you really did look like Frances beneath it. I wanted to know if I could fool Nate. So I decided to take a photograph of you. I wanted to study this later to see if you truly resembled her. However, I couldn't find my camera, and when I returned outside, you were shaken and spoke of seeing three pale faces reflected back in the windowpane. You said also that you heard voices, and I knew then that Frances had been right in her suspicions. Nate had been trying to speak to her and had been watching her more than just the one night agreed.

"But you mentioned the windows and that gave me an idea. So when you were in bed asleep that night, I crept outside and smeared the windows with mud. Should Nate dare to creep close enough to the house and peer in at you, he might see that you weren't really Frances. So I needed to restrict the view of you. I hoped that with the windows covered in dirt and grime, that I could risk sitting you by the window one night, dressed in her clothes. Should he chance peering in, he would believe that he had seen Frances looking happy and contented as she sat with her husband, reading a book."

"You had it all figured out, didn't you?" Winnie sneered with contempt at him.

"No, I didn't," Thaddeus said, his voice soft as he looked at her. "There were a couple of things which happened that I didn't plan for."

"And what were they?" she hissed.

"You started to suspect something was wrong sooner than I imagined you would," he said. "I admit in my arrogance, I thought you would be so relieved to be taken from the streets and thrown into a world of luxuries, that you would have been blinded by what was really happening around you. I didn't think you would be as bright and resourceful as you are."

"Gee, thanks," she said with a fake smile. "I'm truly touched. So what was the other thing you didn't figure in your grand scheme?

Thaddeus sat without saying anything at first, then looking straight at her, he said, "I never thought I would grow as fond for you as I have. I never thought we would become friends..."

"I'm not your friend," Winnie suddenly scoffed.

"That's not true," he whispered. "I admit that when I first asked you to come here I was only thinking of myself and own survival. Now I feel differently. You've made me feel different."

"And do you really think I'm stupid enough to believe that crap?" she snapped back at him.

"But that's the point I'm trying to make," Thaddeus said, his voice still low, still soft. "You're not stupid. You showed me that living locked away in my room isn't the answer. You showed me I can have a new start – you've made me believe that, Winnie."

Looking straight back at him, she said, "And the only way you've made me feel, is scared."

"I didn't mean to."

"You've put me in danger," she said, tears starting to burn in the corners of her eyes. "You are no better than those men who wanted to use me on the streets.

"No, listen to me," Thaddeus begged her. "You were never in any danger. Never. Nate wouldn't hurt you. That's the last thing he would do."

"You mean, he would never hurt Frances," she said, a thin line of tears rolling silently down her face. "But I'm not Frances, and he knows that now."

A heavy silence fell over them, which was only broken by the sound of fingernails tapping against the window.

Chapter Twenty-Nine

"They're back!" Winnie hissed, springing away from the door. She looked at Thaddeus, and his yellow eyes blazed as he instinctively raised his claws. A low snarling sound came from deep within the back of his throat, making him sound like a wolf waiting to strike.

"Lycanthrope!" someone suddenly screeched, and Winnie recognised it to be Nate's voice that she could hear. "Come out, Wolf's-Head. Come out and let us settle the agreement you have broken."

Thaddeus said nothing. He stood back, stooped slightly forward, legs bent at the knees, and snarled. Winnie saw his lips roll back, and his long, pointed teeth glistened. Even though Thaddeus was with her, she felt just as petrified as she had been the night before at the sound of the vampires outside in the moonlight.

"Come out!" Nate roared, and the front door bowed inwards under the weight of him crashing against it.

Thaddeus saw Winnie flinch backwards and throw her hands to her face in fear. "Don't worry; you're quite safe in here. They're vampires."

"That's what scares me," she whispered back at him, eyes wide.

"They can't come in unless we invite them," he snarled back at the door.

As if hearing what he had said, Michelle cooed from beyond the lounge window and said, "You can't hide in there forever, wolf."

Winnie glanced at Thaddeus as Michelle slowly began to drag her long fingernails down the length of the windowpane again. Howling, Thaddeus covered his ears with his claws. Then sinking to his knees, he howled again, his booming cries seeming to make the very foundations of the house shudder. It was as if the sound of Michelle's fingernails being dragged down the windowpane was agonising for him. Hearing his howls of pain, the vampires became excited. Again, Winnie could hear the sound of them scampering up the walls and over the roof. The front door shook in its frame, as all of them began to screech, *"Come out! Come out! Come out!"*

Using the banister, Thaddeus pulled himself to his feet. Then taking Winnie by the shoulders, he looked into her eyes and said, "You are never going to be free of them unless I'm dead."

"But they're vampires, right?" Winnie said back, her mind scrambling. She didn't know much about the whole vampire thing, but she had once seen a film called *Near Dark* with some of the older kids at one of the many care homes she had been passed around. She hadn't seen much from behind the pillow she'd been hiding behind. Winnie saw enough to know that vampires didn't like sunlight. "They'll go away in the morning, won't they? We can escape then."

"If I don't die now, we will both be dead by the morning," he barked at her.

"But how, if they can't come in unless we invite them?" she said. Then, as if in answer to her own question, Winnie suddenly caught the smell of burning. She turned to look at Thaddeus and said, "They're going to burn the house down, aren't they?"

Pulling her close so their faces were just an inch apart, he stared at her and snarled, "You've got to kill me."

"I'm not killing you," she snapped, pulling away.

"Listen to me!" he barked, pulling her close again. "It's the only way you're going to survive this. If you kill me, then they will see you had no feelings for me – that you played no part in Frances's death..."

"But I didn't," Winnie cut in.

"But they don't know that," he said. "But if you kill me..."

"If you want to die, why don't you just let them in," Winnie cut in again.

"If I die from a vampire bite, I burn in Hell for eternity," he said, his yellow eyes seething. "But if you kill me, I pass over peacefully, and there may be a chance I could be with Frances again."

"I'm not going to kill you," she breathed. "You'll have to kill yourself."

"Werewolves can't kill themselves," he said. "It's part of the curse we have to live with." Thaddeus then grabbed her hand, and raced into the lounge.

He went to the fireplace, where he removed one of the large granite stones away, revealing a deep hole. He reached inside with one of his claws. The smell of burning was stronger now. Winnie looked back over her shoulder and could see wisps of black smoke filling the hall, the glow of flames reflecting in the lounge windows.

She looked back at Thaddeus, who was now standing before her with a pistol in his claws.

"What the..." Winnie stared, but before she'd had a chance to finish, Thaddeus had shoved the gun into her hands.

"You must shoot me," he snarled at her. Then, leaping over to the windows, he threw the curtains back and barked, "And they must see you do it if you are going to live."

The gun felt heavy in Winnie's trembling hands. She looked at Thaddeus as he kneeled before her. There was a sound at the windows, and Winnie glanced up to see the three vampires leering excitedly through at them, looking different than they had the night before. Whereas then she had thought they had all looked quite beautiful, now they looked hideous, and she recoiled backwards. With their faces pressed against the windowpane, Winnie thought at first that they had put on those creepy clown masks. In the moonlight and the glow of red and orange flames that now licked the side of the house, she realised that it was, in fact, their own faces she could see. She stared in horror at their eyes, which now looked as if they had sunken into black pits. Their mouths were huge and red. They spread right across their faces, from ear to ear, like a jagged gash. Behind the wide smiles were swollen, black gums and rows of jagged yellow teeth.

Snapping Winnie out of her petrified trance, Thaddeus gripped her wrists and pointed the gun at his own head.

"Shoot me!" he screamed.

"I can't!" Winnie shouted back.

Then, staring up at her, Thaddeus said, "See those faces out there with those giant mouths? Well, if you don't kill me – if they believe you are a part of all of this – they will rip you to pieces with those mouths. They will suck the flesh from your body. They will rip your heart out and share it between them."

Even though Thaddeus had hold of her wrists, her hands shook so much, the end of the barrel kept sliding across his forehead where he had placed it. "Why didn't you get Frances to kill you?" Winnie whispered, her lips trembling. "If you loved each other so much, why didn't she kill you so you could be together?"

Then opening his eyes, Thaddeus stared up into hers and said, "I can't be killed by someone who loves me."

Winnie looked back over her shoulder and could see the hallway was now a wall of thick, dense, black smoke. It smelt acrid and was choking. She glanced at the window where the vampires, with their hideous faces, stared excitedly in at her. She could hear the sound of the eaves above her snapping and hissing as flames took hold of them. She looked down at Thaddeus.

"I'm sorry for making you a part of this," he whispered, then closed his eyes. "Shoot me."

With tears streaming from her eyes, Winnie closed them and placed her finger on the trigger.

Chapter Thirty

"I'm not going to kill you," she whispered down at Thaddeus, and pulled her hands free of the gun.

"You must..." Thaddeus started.

But Winnie had turned and fled, disappearing into the bank of black smoke that filled the hallway and was now wafting up the stairs. With her hand over her mouth and nose, Winnie raced through the hall. The air felt burning hot as it touched her face, hair, and hands. Coughing and choking, she made her way into the kitchen. Orange flames danced up the walls and across the ceiling. Peering through her fingers, Winnie tried to see through the intoxicating smoke and flames. Crouched low, she stumbled across the kitchen, striking the corner of the table with her thigh. She cried out in pain, sucking in a throat full of black air. The smoke hit the back of her throat, and it felt scorching hot. Winnie tried to cough the smoke up out of her lungs, tears streaming from her eyes, and drool hanging from her mouth and nose. She dropped to her hands and knees, and feeling as if she were going lose consciousness, she crawled across the kitchen floor. On the other side of the room, she reached up and gripped the edge of the sink. She pulled herself up, and trying desperately not to breathe in, she climbed onto the counter. Through the window she had cleaned, she could see the fields stretching away at the back of the house towards the sea.

With the window seeming to soar before her burning eyes, she hoisted it open. Sucking in a mouthful of cold night air like a drowning fish, she forced her way through the open window. Winnie hung upside down momentarily, her jeans snagging on the window lock. Crying out, she wriggled her leg left and right, desperate to free herself before the smoke and fire took her, or the vampires realised that she was making her escape.

At the front of the house, Michelle heard Winnie cry out. With her long blue hair fanning out behind her, and her jagged teeth gleaming in the light from the flames, she raced towards the back of the house. Nate stared through the window at Thaddeus, who still knelt on the floor. He wasn't interested in the girl, the Frances imposter; Claude and Michelle could fuck with her. Nate wanted Thaddeus. The hatred he felt inside for the wolf burnt as greedily and as hot as the flames which now clawed their way up the front of the house. He would avenge Frances's death. He owed it to her, to Nicodemus, but more importantly, to himself.

No one could have known the torment he had lived through for the last three hundred years. Each day and night, every second had been consumed with the thought of his beloved Frances sharing her bed, her life, her soul, with a Lycanthrope. Had anyone known the pain he had felt as he watched Frances from afar, once a year, as she stood alone for him in the moonlight? Did they know that the anguish he felt at being forbidden to talk to her, to hold her? It had driven him half-mad with jealously and rage. However, it was more than that – it was the fear he felt in his heart for her. He knew that Thaddeus would one day kill her. Nate knew in his heart that Thaddeus was only keeping her alive to torture him. How could any man live a happy life, knowing that the person they loved, the person they would give their life for, was with another?

As Nate stood amongst the smoke and flames and stared in at Thaddeus on his knees, he remembered the terrible nights he watched Frances in the moonlight, knowing that she would soon be returning to the Lycanthrope's bed, where it would make love to her. Nate would sit with his head in his hands as he pictured the wolf's claws caressing her beautiful body. He could hear Frances crying out with pleasure. Some nights, Nate hated Frances as much as the wolf. How could she have fallen in love with him? But the wolf had tricked her, bewitched her. Nate had heard that some Lycanthrope could do that. So his hatred for Frances would melt away, and only grow stronger for the wolf. It had become like a poison inside of him, which seethed through his veins and blackened his heart. Tonight, at last, Nate would unleash that fury eating away inside of him, and kill the wolf. At last he would be able to take the wolf's head back to his home, hidden deep within the Carpathian Mountains, and hand it to Nicodemus. The last of the Lycanthrope would be dead. Their species snuffed out of existence, like a candle flame.

Thaddeus looked at the thick, black smoke rapidly coming towards him, then at the window. He saw Nate staring back at him, his eyes blood-red with fury. He would have to wait, Thaddeus thought. Nate could have him, but first he had to get Winnie to safety. He had done terrible things to get Winnie into this, and she had been right – he had put her life in danger. Before he died, before he was sent back to Hell where he knew perhaps he deserved to be, he wanted to help Winnie escape. Thaddeus wanted to do that one last thing. Not because he felt he had to, not because he thought he might be looked more favourable upon in the next life – he had done enough to know that would never happen – but because he did have feelings for her. However unexpected those feelings had been, however sudden they had grown inside him, he did hope that somewhere inside of her, she felt the same. Winnie hadn't been able to kill him, no more than Frances would have been able to.

He looked back through the window at Nate, and flashing his teeth and snarling, Thaddeus leapt into the smoke in search of Winnie.

Chapter Thirty-One

Winnie pulled her leg free from the lock and collapsed in a heap in the grass beneath the window. Gasping for air, she knew she didn't have long to put as much distance between her and the house. With mud and grass seeping beneath her fingernails, Winnie clawed forward, her chest heaving up and down as she tried desperately to catch her breath. With her head and lungs beginning to clear, Winnie got to her feet. Stumbling forward like a drunk, she made her way into the dark and towards the sea. She could hear the waves crashing against the cliffs in the distance, hoping that she might be able to find someplace to hide amongst the rocks.

Winnie glanced back over her shoulder in panic, just to make sure she wasn't being followed. The huge house looked awash with flames. They twisted and ravaged their way across the roof and up the walls. Thick plumes of smoke twisted up into the night, blocking out the moon like a black cloud. Then she saw the vampire, Claude leap from the burning roof. Even without the light of the moon, his razor-sharp teeth glistened in his huge, twisted mouth. He landed in the long grass and came towards her. Winnie spun around, and with her lungs screaming for more clean air, she raced away. With arms pumping up and down by her sides, and her heart slamming in her chest, Winnie frantically pushed herself forward. She could hear the sound of racing footsteps behind her. How had he covered the distance between them so quickly? Her mind screamed. Again she looked back and saw Claude's grotesque face looming out of the darkness at her. With a scream tearing its way up her throat, Winnie stumbled backwards and onto the ground with a thump. What little good air was in her lungs was forced out of her. Eyes wide with terror, Winnie kicked out at him.

"Get away from me!" she screamed, but her voice came out sounding like an out of breath gasp.

Claude looked down at her. Watching Winnie try and defend herself excited him. He had longed for one of the females to fight back. The feeding would be so sweet. Her heart would still be racing fast as he plucked it from her chest. The thought of her hot blood pumping into his mouth made him shudder with expectant pleasure.

Suddenly he lunged at her, and then pulled back again, like he was teasing Winnie. She scrambled backwards, thrashing out with her arms and legs. He lunged again, and then pulled back. He was enjoying watching her panic. Claude loved seeing the terror in her eyes. It was beautiful.

"Don't hurt me!" she screamed.

He loved hearing her say that, because it was so dumb. Of course he was going to hurt her. He was going to teach her what pain was.

Winnie dug the heels of her trainers into the ground and pushed herself away from him. He lunged at her again, his ragged claws just inches from her eyes. Then he was joined by another. Michelle suddenly appeared beside Claude like a flickering shadow. Her long, blue hair flowed out behind her, like a streak of lightning. This close, Winnie could see that Michelle's mouth looked as if someone had slit her face open. Her lips looked like two slices of raw meat. Her dead, black eyes stared down at Winnie.

"What are you waiting for, Claude?" she whispered. "Take her."

Claude couldn't bear the sense of excitement and urgency he felt inside of him any longer. So with his long, white claws clacking together like a set of knives, he lowered himself over Winnie.

Seeing this, Winnie scrambled backwards and both vampires laughed. Suddenly, she heard another sound behind their shrieks of joy. It was the sound of howling. A black shadow streaked before her eyes. Then both Claude and Michelle flew backwards off their feet and into the air. The black shadow seemed to pause – take form – before her. It was Thaddeus. He looked back at her, his eyes bright yellow, messy hair blowing in the wind, and claws swinging by his sides.

"Okay?" he asked Winnie.

"Okay," she whispered.

Before she could say anything else, he was leaping through the air and swiping at Michelle and Claude with his claws. His long, curled fingernails shone like silver as they sliced through the air. He howled so loud that the ground shook beneath Winnie. Pulling herself up onto her elbows, she watched in horror as Thaddeus clattered into Claude, sending them both sprawling to the ground. With his muscular arms just a blur in the moonlight, Thaddeus slashed, tore, and ripped at the vampire screeching in agony beneath him. Within seconds Thaddeus had opened up Claude's stomach, throwing lengths of oily black entrails into the air. Claude made a gargling noise as if being strangled. Winnie turned away as Thaddeus drove his claws into the vampire's throat. Something heavy thudded into the ground next to Winnie. Peeking through her fingers, she looked with revulsion at a long pointed-looking slab of meat, which had landed just inches from her. It twitched like a giant worm, and Winnie got up and ran as she realised it was Claude's tongue she could see wriggling about in the grass.

With the sound of Claude's agonising shrieks, and Thaddeus's booming howls in her ears, Winnie failed to hear Michelle racing up behind her. It wasn't until the vampire had leapt onto her back that Winnie realised that Michelle had been charging after her. Winnie spun around as Michelle dug her claws into her shoulders. Winnie screamed out in pain. The vampire's claws felt like ten burning daggers slicing into her flesh.

"Get the fuck off me, bitch!" Winnie screamed, bucking like a donkey, desperate to throw Michelle free.

But the vampire's grip was unbreakable. Winnie threw herself backwards, crushing Michelle beneath her. The vampire shrieked, withdrawing her claws from Winnie as she tried to free herself from beneath. The pain of the claws being withdrawn from her flesh was just as painful as them going in, and a blinding bolt of pain shot through her shoulders and into Winnie's brain. In agony, she rolled off Michelle onto her hands and knees, and tried to get to her feet. The vampire had only been momentarily stunned, and pouncing to her feet, she kicked out at Winnie and sent her sprawling into the ground. Winnie's chin struck a rock jutting out of the grass, and a jet of blood burst from the gash it had made in her face. With the air now full of the sweet smell of blood, Michelle ran her tongue over her raw-looking lips and threw herself at Winnie.

She rolled over just in time to see the vampire's fangs come rushing out of the darkness at her. Winnie threw her hands in front of her face, and she felt Michelle's fangs sink into her forearm. The pain, like before was excruciating, and Winnie thought she might just puke. With bile burning in the back of her throat, Winnie screamed in pain as she pulled her arm free of Michelle's jaws. Blood sprayed into the air, covering Winnie's face with her own blood. With her arm spurting a constant stream of thick, black blood, she tried to beat off Michelle, who lunged at her over and over again.

Screaming, she tried to fight the vampire off, but Winnie knew it was only a matter of seconds before she became too consumed with pain to fight on. Then, with Michelle's hideous face swimming before her, Winnie thought she saw a flash of red cloth go racing past. If Michelle hadn't seen it, she must have felt something, as she momentarily looked in the direction that the red streak had gone. With the vampire's head turned away, Winnie seized the moment and drove both sets of her fingernails into the creature's eyes. Michelle's eyeballs felt soft and wet beneath Winnie's fingernails. Knowing that this was her last chance, she drove her fingers as far and as deep as she could into the vampire's eyes. One of them squirted onto Michelle's cheek in a thick, gloopy white-coloured mess. It felt hot as it ran over the back of Winnie's hand and down the length of her wrist.

Twisting her back like a corkscrew, the vampire screeched in agony as Winnie pulled her fingernails from her eye sockets. "I'm blind!" she screamed. "I'm fucking blind!"

"And I'm bleeding!" Winnie roared back scrambling to her feet. Holding her arm tightly to her chest, to try and slow the blood gushing from the rips in her flesh, she watched Michelle stagger blindly about.

"*I'm blind!*" she screamed again, her long, blue hair blowing in the wind.

"No, you're dead," somebody howled from the darkness.

Before Winnie truly knew what was happening, Thaddeus had bounded like a giant hound from the dark. With one fleeting swipe of his claw, Michelle's head was spinning away through the air. Her torso stood where it was, twitched, and then toppled over. Thaddeus glanced at Winnie. His shirt had been torn free, and bloody streaks covered his chest. His arms looked taut, and he flexed his claws open and closed.

"I know what you're thinking," he snarled at Winnie.

She looked back at him and nodded.

"Then do it, Winnie," he barked at her. "Run! Run! Run! And never look back!"

Looking at him one last time, dripping with blood in the moonlight, Winnie turned and ran.

Chapter Thirty-Two

With the vampire's blood hot beneath his long fingernails, Thaddeus stood and looked at his burning house in the distance. It had been consumed by flames and it burnt like a torch on the horizon. Clouds of black smoke billowed up into the night sky. He knew whether it burnt to the ground or not, he would never be able to return there. His life in Cornwall was over. His life was over. He waited, drenched by moonlight. He wanted Nate to find him. He wanted it to be over at last.

Then, silhouetted by the red of the flames in the distance, he saw Nate coming across the fields towards him. With his claws hanging low by his sides, he breathed deeply and waited for the inevitable. He couldn't kill himself. Winnie, just like Frances, hadn't been able to do so either, but for the same reasons, he couldn't be sure. That didn't matter now. He watched Nate approach him, each step slow and deliberate, as if he were savouring every moment.

The thought of dying now didn't matter. He could kill Nate as easily as he had killed the others. What was the point? There would only be others. Word would soon get back to Nicodemus that his daughter was dead, killed by the wolf. Enraged with grief, and feeling betrayed, he would only send more, who would hunt him down. Thaddeus knew that it was over. He couldn't go on moving from one place to another, living a life where he was constantly looking back over his shoulder, reading mountains of foreign newspapers, trying to work out where his enemies would come from next. That wasn't a life – that was a living hell. He had tried to trick them and what had he achieved? For his own selfish gain, he had deceived a young girl, he had brought a young girl to his home, placed her in mortal danger and what for? So he could put off the inevitable for another year – another three or four perhaps? They would have caught up with him soon enough, and even if he had managed to trick Winnie into staying with him all that time, they would have killed her, too.

He knew he had felt something for her, however small, but to let those feelings grow and mature would have been another selfish act on his part. She would have exchanged one life of constant running for another. Winnie was free now, not of her own ghosts, but of his.

As Thaddeus watched Nate take his last few steps towards him, and as they stood eye to eye at last, Thaddeus, dropped to his knees and lowered his head.

"If you truly felt anything for Frances, make this quick for me," Thaddeus said. "As I sat and watched her fade away, we both knew this moment would eventually come. She wouldn't have wanted me to suffer." He then reached into the back of his waistband and removed the gun he had earlier tried to get Winnie to kill him with. Looking up into Nate's dead black eyes, he offered him the gun.

Nate slowly took the gun and turned it over in his hands. "A murderer and coward," he sneered. "A true Lycanthrope."

"I'm neither," Thaddeus whispered to himself more than to his executioner.

Nate heard him all the same, and whipped him across the side of the face with the butt of the gun. Thaddeus howled in pain, as his head rocked to the left.

Throwing the gun into the grass, Nate towered over Thaddeus and said, "I've waited three hundred years for this moment. *Three hundred years!*" he screeched, spit flying from his lips and spraying Thaddeus's naked chest. "And for every one of those days, I've tormented myself – driven myself half-mad - thinking of how when I sink my fangs into your putrid heart, I want to feel it still beating."

"Whatever you think happened to Frances, I'm not going to spend my last few moments trying to convince you otherwise," Thaddeus said calmly, "we loved each other more than you'll ever know."

"You don't have the faintest idea what true love is, wolf!" Nate screeched at him. "You're nothing but an animal. It was I who truly loved Frances."

Then, slowly lifting his head, Thaddeus looked into Nate's eyes. "If you truly had loved Frances, you wouldn't have asked her to stand in the moonlight. You would have set her free."

With a rage which paled anything he had felt before, Nate raised his claws in the air and brought them slicing down. Thaddeus threw back his head, exposing his neck, waiting for the vampire's claws to slice open his throat and at last set him free. Thaddeus didn't know what came first, the warm splatter of blood across his upturned face, or the sound of the gun firing.

.

Chapter Thirty-Three

Thaddeus opened one eye to see Nate slump face first into the ground. He then opened the other, and saw Winnie standing with the gun wavering in her trembling hands. Blood and lumps of Nate's brain slid done the length of Thaddeus's face like giant black tears. He armed them away, unable to take his eyes off Winnie.

"What have you done?" he howled.

"Saved your life," Winnie breathed, dropping the gun as if it now carried some disease she might catch.

"Why?" he barked. "After everything I have put you through."

"Because you saved my life," Winnie whispered, holding her bleeding arm against her chest.

"But you haven't saved my life, Winnie," he snarled at her.

"What are you talking about?" she asked, unable to figure out why he seemed so angry. Then, looking at the scattered remains of the vampires, she added, "They're dead, aren't they?"

"*They're* dead," Thaddeus growled. "But there will be others. It won't take long for Nicodemus to figure out what went on here. Just like Nate, he will come after me to avenge the death of Frances."

"I'm sorry," Winnie said, looking back at the house which was now nothing more than just a raging inferno.

"I had set you free. Why did you come back for me?" Thaddeus barked at her.

"Because you said we were friends," she breathed, looking back at him. "That's what friends do, isn't it?"

Thaddeus looked back at her, not knowing what to say or do. With his temper calming, and seeing the blood funnelling from the cut in Winnie's face and leaking down her arm, he went to her and took her in his arms.

Slowly, Winnie folded her arms around him and held onto Thaddeus. Resting her tired head against his shoulder, Winnie looked into the distance. Not knowing whether to laugh or cry, she saw a little figure wearing a blood-red coat standing atop a grassy knoll in the distance.

Ruby Little raised one pale hand into the air and slowly beckoned Winnie with it.

"I don't know what we do now," Thaddeus whispered into Winnie's ear as he held her.

"We do what I do best," she whispered back. "We *run*."

Winnie glanced up at the grassy knoll again, but Ruby Little had gone. In her place, was a pool of moonlight.

Moonbeam

Book two in the Moon Trilogy
Coming soon!

Also available by Tim O'Rourke
'Vampire Shift' (Kiera Hudson Series One Book 1)
'Vampire Wake' (Kiera Hudson Series One Book 2)
'Vampire Hunt' (Kiera Hudson Series One Book 3)
'Vampire Breed' Kiera Hudson Series One Book 4)
'Wolf House' (Kiera Hudson Series One Book 4.5)
'Vampire Hollows' (Kiera Hudson Series One Book 5)
'Dead Flesh' (Kiera Hudson Series Two Book 1)
'Dead Night' (Kiera Hudson Series Two Book 1.5)
'Dead Angels' (Kiera Hudson Series Two book 2)
'Black Hill Farm' (Book 1)
'Black Hill Farm: Andy's Diary' (Book 1)
'Doorways' (The Doorways Trilogy Book 1)
'The League of Doorways' (The Doorways Trilogy Book 2)
'Cowgirls & Vampires' (Book 1)
'Moonlight' (The Moon Trilogy Book 1)

About the Author
Working away in the dead of night, Tim has written many short stories, plays and novels. Tim is the author of the bestselling 'Kiera Hudson series', the two paranormal romance books entitled 'Black Hill Farm' and the 'Doorways' Trilogy.

Tim is currently working on his new series 'Cowgirls & Vampires'. The first book is now available.

Tim's interests other than writing, include watching South Park, Vampire Diaries, True Blood and listening to Pitbull,

LMFAO, Jennifer Lopez, David Guetta, Bruno Mars, Rihanna and Adele. Tim is never happier than when reading The Twilight Series, Vampire Diaries and writing his own Vampire series 'Kiera Hudson'.

Don't be shy; feel free to contact Tim at Ravenwoodgreys@aol.com - Tim would love to hear from you. Website: www.Ravenwoodgreys.com

.

2961634R00083

Printed in Great Britain
by Amazon.co.uk, Ltd.,
Marston Gate.